Ambush at Yuma's Chimney

AMBUSH AT YUMA'S CHIMNEY

NELSON NYE

THORNDIKE
CHIVERS

This Large Print edition is published by Thorndike Press, Waterville, Maine, USA and by AudioGO Ltd, Bath, England.
Thorndike Press, a part of Gale, Cengage Learning.
The text of this Large Print edition is unabridged.
Other aspects of the book may vary from the original edition.
Set in 16 pt. Plantin.

LIBRARY OF CONGRESS CATALOGING-IN-PUBLICATION DATA

Nye, Nelson C. (Nelson Coral), 1907–
  Ambush at Yuma's Chimney / by Nelson Nye. — Large print ed.
    p. cm. — (Thorndike Press large print western)
  ISBN-13: 978-1-4104-4098-3 (hardcover)
  ISBN-10: 1-4104-4098-2 (hardcover)
  1. Large type books. I. Title.
PS3527.Y33.A43 2011
813'.54—dc23   2011021830

BRITISH LIBRARY CATALOGUING-IN-PUBLICATION DATA AVAILABLE

Published in 2011 in the U.S. by arrangement with Golden West Literary Agency.
Published in 2012 in the U.K. by arrangement with Golden West Literary Agency.

U.K. Hardcover: 978 1 445 86047 3 (Chivers Large Print)
U.K. Softcover: 978 1 445 86048 0 (Camden Large Print)

Printed in the United States of America
1 2 3 4 5 6 7 15 14 13 12 11

AUTHOR'S NOTE

For the factual aspects of this novel, the author is indebted first of all to Nova Alderson, Reference Librarian of the Arizona Pioneers' Historical Society, who deeply delved among antiquarian documents and dusty records, unearthing several discoveries, people and placenames, not generally heretofore acknowledged. I would like also to admit benefits obtained from *Coronado's Children* by the late J. Frank Dobie and much additional help provided by the labors of John D. Gilchriese, Field Historian of the University of Arizona.

— NELSON NYE
Tucson, 1965

5

I

Mountain wind, crying through the brush, came down off the peaks with the scent of winter, though heat still lay like a smoky film over the Camp Grant flats where the water of the San Pedro River usually surged across the sands of Arivaipa Creek. Both beds were now dry as a lime-burner's hat. Barney Olds, peering red-eyed back across a sweat-rimed shoulder at the dust storm boiling over his backtrail, shook an angry fist and swore.

He'd got off those sinks just about in time. Bloody Head's Apaches, had they got their hands on him, would have cooked him sure! It was the only good thing he could say for his luck and for once he was glad to be in sight of the post. He spat out a stringer of cottony grit and, scowling into the cinnamon face of his burro, spat again. "Pammy, dang it, we're both gettin' old," he croaked, peering round at the piles of loose stones heaped here and yon where other poor devils had lost their hair.

Not a few of these cairns were topped by rude crosses made from the stalks of mescal and Spanish dagger and these, he thought, looked loneliest of all. It was time he got out of this golrammed country, and nobody knew it more surely than Olds.

The need was like a hound on his trail, sniffling and snapping, badgering him without letup, sometimes in its terrifying persistence rousting him out of a sound snoring sleep. A feller had to stay on his toes in this country. Accidents or ambush inevitably took care of fools who didn't.

Sure, a man hated to let go of a thing he'd set his teeth in, but he would hate a mighty more to leave his bones in this desert, and Olds was no nearer now to finding Yuma's Chimney than he had been at the beginning.

Five years of looking, of following a burro's tail through the broiling hell of these burning wastes, and nothing to show for it but a skinful of wrinkles!

It was the sand. That's what it was — the golrammed sand! Never constant, always shifting, covering at night what it bared during the day, changing, altered by every wind that ripped across it. He could have camped forty times atop that chimney and never known it!

Five years of grubstakes had worn out his welcome.

The scoffing he could take, but even fools had to eat, and the pained looks, the resentful frowns that came over the faces of substantial citizens whenever he hove into sight anymore, told louder than words how near he was to the end of his string. Even the greediest no longer could stomach him, and Sully — George Sullivan, the grubstake king who owned half of Tucson — had bluntly told him when he'd took off this last trip, if he didn't find it this time not to bother coming back.

If there was one single thing a feller could count on it was the prevalent belief a man had sure enough had it when Lucky George turned loose of him.

And it wasn't just Tucson. All over the cactus he'd be held a bad risk once the word got around he'd come back empty-handed. Hard luck in this country flew like the wind.

Olds wasn't short on lies but after five years of it who would believe him? They all knew Sully had kept him going, and George — even if prevailed upon one more final time — would expect something solider than words to stand good for him.

There wasn't one place he could talk up a stake. At Bisbee or Benson folks wouldn't give him the time of day, and that marshal at Fairbank would jug him on sight. Even at Willcox they had him pegged for a bum — him, Barney Olds, who scarcely six years ago had been acclaimed a national hero!

Tagging his burro up the dusty road toward the post's main gate, Barney scanned his prospects and lugubriously sighed, hard up as any skinny-necked Christian in the land of the Philistines. Most places, fame wouldn't even wet his whistle. The sutler's bar at this isolated post was the only dive he could still raise a drink — and not even there if the papers had reached them.

He had seen one last week, a copy of *The Epitaph* — and a regular kiss of death it had been. Right on the front page in searing black letters he had read his own name under the caption NOT RESPONSIBLE. Lucky George had publicly washed his hands of him.

He could still probably wangle a job playing scout for Feltenmeyer's cavalry, but work of that nature held little appeal to a man grown accustomed to thinking in terms of unlimited wealth. If only, by grab, he could have latched onto that chimney!

Five years of believing it just over the next

ridge made scouting look like the ass-end of nothing. He could see it now, a vertical ore shoot buried in sand, thick as a man's body, pretty near solid gold! Hard to put out of mind, harder still to give up. It was out there somewhere — *it had to be.* Even the craziest of those stories couldn't have got going without *some* truth!

It was scarcely twenty years back when that Army officer, that bald-faced lieutenant from West Point remembered now only as "Yuma," had been sent as acting-quartermaster to Fort Yuma on the Colorado. He had had supervision of all supplies, not only for his own post but for others strung out across this vast spread of country. The tonnage handled was enormous, supplies being paid for by vouchers drawn on the quartermaster-general's West Coast office. Fallen under the sway of dishonest contractors, the lieutenant known as Yuma had been court-martialed and discharged from the service.

Educated, of gentle breeding and considerable pride, Yuma had keenly felt his disgrace, had finally taken refuge among the Yuma Indians. Chief of these was Pascual, a gaunt man with a prodigious nose from which dangled an ornament made of white bone. His power over the tribe was absolute, his subjects living off the fat of the land. In due course he gave one of his loveliest daughters to the cashiered lieutenant and Yuma, after their marriage, became an adopted member of the tribe.

Yuma then went into business, setting up a trading post. His adopted relatives enjoyed the good will of the scattered Apache tribes and, with his wife for protection, Yuma was free to go where he would. With mules heavily loaded with things most desired by this warrior people, Yuma and his Indian wife penetrated places never before seen by a white man. Life was congenial, his affairs prospered, everywhere he went he found the Indians affable.

From his wife and other persons he discovered that the Arivaipas had a golden horde from which they had been known to barter jewelry rock. Its whereabouts, of course, was a fiercely guarded secret but, presuming now upon the esteem in which his own tribe held him and his spreading reputation among affiliated tribes, he made cautiously crafty overtures to the chief of these Arivaipas, offering many fine gifts for a glimpse of the cache.

Upshot was that shortly after daybreak on a fateful morning the chief and Yuma took off afoot with rifles, presumably on a hunting expedition. Striking out in a northerly direction they climbed a ridge along which they moved for perhaps three miles. Against the side of a gulch, well up from its bed, the chief suddenly stopped. Yuma saw a crater-like hollow, not at all conspicuous, possibly five or more feet in diameter, heavily rimmed with stones.

"Here," said the chief, peering about.

Yuma dropped into the depression, got out his knife and started to dig. It wasn't very long before he struck ore, finally managing to hack off a handful. He shook all over he was so excited. The ore was rose quartz, fatly veined with gold, jewelry rock of the rarest kind. Even then, probably, Yuma was figuring behind guarded cheeks how best to get away with this bonanza.

After filling the hole and erasing all sign of his activities, Yuma and the chief went off to bag some game. But not before the erstwhile lieutenant took careful note of the ground roundabout, the general lay of the land and the fact that the gulch below them headed only scant rods beyond. This terrain, as he subsequently described it, was so rocky and badly broken up that no one unaware of the secret would be likely to stumble onto it. The chief earnestly cautioned him to tell no one, lest he be killed for his knowledge.

Barney knew enough about mining to realize from the sample he had seen that the chimney might easily produce ore valued at a million or more dollars in a very short while at practically no expense — if a man could come at it.

Sometime later, at Tucson, Yuma got in touch with a young freighter named Crittenden who was currently engaged in hauling ore from the mining camps to Fort Yuma, at which point it was loaded aboard steamers. Crittenden, having fallen in with his plan, made preparations to explore the chimney.

Quitting the dust of Tucson late one evening the conspirators, mounted on desert bred horses, rode all night, and early next morning arrived at Camp Grant. After resting till dark they struck off down the San Pedro, covering approximately ten miles and then waiting for daybreak, at which time, remounting, they began to climb west. The terrain was so steeply rough they were forced much of the time to get off and walk, leading their horses, pretty grueling work considering the heat that hung over this region.

Hours later they'd come into the gulch up which the chief had taken the lieutenant.

Yuma found the depression. Employing pick and shovel, in two hours time they broke loose about thirty pounds, packing only the choicest pieces. Burying their tools and all trace of their labors, the pair, riding all night, struck out for Tucson, swinging wide of Camp Grant and the San Pedro Valley. Working down the west slope of the mountains and crossing a trackless basin they came into Tucson just as first light was breaking over the town.

One of the things Barney had repeatedly tried during the years of his own search was to discover how far, in this fashion, you could ride in one night — and he still didn't know. He'd been compelled in these attempts to start out from Tucson and had never wound up in the same place twice. He *had* found the basin, but this had not proved to be much of a help. He could not even be sure the yarn, as he had it, had not been deliberately concocted to conceal the true facts. He had even put in the bulk of one winter gophering that basin and every gulch that led off it.

With the ore crushed — all but the few chunks preserved as samples — it turned out that from less than the original thirty pounds $1200 worth of gold was extracted. The whole town went wild when news of this fabulous strike leaked out.

Afraid to return during this high fever of excitement, suspicious of everyone who accosted them, the partners decided to put off for a while any idea of returning to their cache. Crittenden went back to his freighting. Yuma, again accompanied by his Indian wife, went into the desert a hundred miles west of Tucson on a trading venture among the Papagoes.

This was the tribe which, under Father Kino, had built San Xavier del Bac on the Santa Cruz River south of the Old Pueblo, one of the finest missions in the whole Southwest. These Papagoes, known as the earliest Christianized Indians, were mostly farmers and ranchers, traditionally friendly toward the squabbling whites. They had suffered long at the hands of Apaches and looked upon the Yumas as Apache allies.

It was an everlasting puzzle why the cashiered lieutenant should have taken his Yuma wife among them, or why she would have gone. There was ample proof, however, that both Yuma and his recent bride had indeed gone off with several hundred pounds of trade goods into the lands of the Papagoes and were never seen again.

Crittenden, after long weeks of waiting for his partner's return, finally gave Yuma up for dead and prepared to re-visit the partnership mine. He set out alone, intending to post notice of their discovery, thus establishing legal title. He went by way of their original route, spending two days at Camp Grant where he was brash enough to make no secret of his present mission. He rode an exceptionally fine horse which was much admired. Letting it be known he could be expected back before nightfall, he left the cavalry post early in the morning of the third day and was never again seen alive by the officer personnel.

All this had come out during subsequent investigations. Everyone knew this much about the business. The yarn long since had become common property and others ahead of Olds had vigorously probed the general vicinity, not a few of these leaving their bones out there or losing their hair to paint-smeared renegades presumed to be followers of Bloody Head.

It was no place for weak hearts or blundering greenhorns.

Three days after Crittenden had quit Camp Grant a cavalry patrol attempting to track him had found his thirst-crazed horse entangled in a picket rope on the west flank of the San Pedro wash some ten miles north of the post and not far from the base of a broken range of mountains. Discovered near the horse were Crittenden's saddle and bridle. The finest trackers available scoured the surrounding region for days, even finding where the freighter had scaled the mountain afoot. But they didn't find him or his rifle. It was common belief he'd been surprised by Apaches and had paid for this carelessness in the customary manner.

Shortly after this a band of possibly one hundred Papagoes, led by a handful of Americans and Mexicans from Tucson, surprised the Arivaipa Apaches in their camp and butchered the lot, men, women and children. This is known to history as the Camp Grant Massacre, and took place in 1871. All the tribe wasn't on hand and Bloody Head's raiders had been formed from the survivors. Fierce and vengeful, they had successfully eluded all attempts of the cavalry to apprehend them and, save for Barney Olds' forays, they had effectively discouraged further search for the hidden chimney. Nor had they overlooked Barney; they had come today within short yards of putting an end to him. Except for that sandstorm they would certainly have caught him.

II

The weight of the sun was like an iron fist in the blinding glare that engulfed the parade ground as she watched the stage through its lift of dust cut around a cramped circle and with a hard run of hoofs disappear through the gate.

In the confusion of her thoughts she could almost hear the crackle of burned bridges, and in this moment of panic the miles she had put between herself and Tucson seemed as reproachful as anything she had known. No proper young lady would *ever* have given in to so hoydenish an impulse.

A parched grin tugged apart the stiffness of rouged lips and some of her fright fell away at the absurdity of the comparison. A "proper armful" would be a deal nearer the truth to the patrons of the White Horse Bar. Through the familiarities of nightly routine in the hard life she'd come from she had at any rate managed to stay aloof from any man and, till now at least, had bleakly fashioned her existence along lines dictated by the harsh necessity of having to be practical.

She hoped for a trade, but not even now was she considering settling for anything less than legal marriage performed by a bonafide priest. True, she was putting herself right out on a limb where there'd be plenty of wind and a considerable drop — but not without examining it carefully beforehand. She knew the game she stalked. Hard won experience would determine how to trap it if she got any kind of break.

Hers was not any spur-of-the-moment decision. She had thought a long time about its ramifications, determined to get clear while she still had convertible assets. Since the age of eleven she had been on her own. She had looks and youth, and had seen quite enough in the interim to realize such advantages were not indestructible.

She'd been the only person to quit the stage here and the corporal, hoisting the bulge of his mailsack, let speculative eyes run considerably over her. His lips stretched in a grin. Carmella lifted her chin.

"If you're hunting Suds Row," he said, the grin bolder, "it's right over there," and pointed.

Her eyes did not follow the lift of his hand. With that jaw and those burnsides there were women, she supposed, who might think him handsome. She said, "Indeed?" then coolly ignored him to gaze into the southern distance where scriggles of dust whirled and danced in the sun.

She heard the uncertain shift of his feet. He was turning away when she said, "Maybe you could tell me where to find Barney Olds?"

The trooper's stare crawled over her again. "Olds . . . ?" he said, jaw dropped, and snorted. But, eyes digging into her, he seemed forced to conclude she must really have been serious. Then, still not sure, he said owl-eyed: "Ever git downwind of him? Honey, you kin do better than a one-armed ol' has-been —"

Breaking off at the look of her he hurriedly back-pedaled, but it was plain she wasn't about to pull up. With the sparks shooting out of her she took hold of her parasol like it was a club. The sight was too much for him — he wasn't of the breed who cared for tigers in their tanks. Whirling, still hugging his mailsack, he took off for headquarters like a ruptured duck.

Carmella, bristling, went back to her luggage.

The only actual glimpse she'd ever caught of the man had been a back view of him departing through the White Horse's batwings one night as she'd been coming down the stairs. She'd only known it was Olds because of the talk and he had certainly looked to be all there then.

She got so lost in thought she failed to note the approach of footsteps and was considerably startled when a voice gruffly inquired, "Can I help you, miss?"

Spinning about, eyes lifting, she found herself confronted by an iron-gray face squarely set beneath the hat of an officer of cavalry. There was an air of authority about him which was infinitely comforting. "I'm looking for Mr. Olds," she said, and saw him rub at his chin perplexedly.

"I . . . ah —" His widening eyes peered more intently at her as though discovering things not previously noticed. "That wouldn't be *Barney* Olds, would it?" and she nodded, wondering.

The officer scrubbed his chin more vigorously. "Afraid Olds isn't at the post right now. I suppose it's terribly important, or . . . ?"

"It is to me," she declared, batting her eyes as though bravely determined to hold back the tears. "If you were a young girl left alone in the world . . ." She paused, overcome, then in a frail, desperate voice managed painfully to say: "He gave me every reason to believe —" and stopped. "When he wrote, enclosing stage fare, asking me to be here on the twenty-ninth, I naturally supposed . . . This *is* the twenty-ninth, isn't it?"

He took off his hat to scratch around through gray hair. "I believe it is." He said, attempting to reassure her, "If Olds said the twenty-ninth I imagine he will make every effort to be here. . . ." But behind his stiff cheeks he wasn't sure of that at all, and some of this uncertainty crept into the words. He said abruptly, realizing this: "I'm sure Mrs. Feltenmeyer — my wife, that is, will be delighted to extend you the hospitality of our quarters until such time as —"

"You mean he's out with a patrol?"

The colonel looked dumbfounded.

She watched him through the curl of dark lashes. Then, sighing, declared briskly: "He's told me how kind and thoughtful you are, always worrying about the men, and how dependent you are on his services as scout — but I mustn't be a nuisance. I'll just wait in the shade. . . ."

"Nonsense!" Feltenmeyer said, a little flushed, his tone strongly colored by irritation and embarrassment. "My wife will be glad to have you. Life can get pretty bleak out here. Your company could do her a world of good." He picked up her carpet bag, surprised at its lightness. "I don't believe, young lady, I've had the pleasure of your name."

"I'm Carmella — Carmella Ramirez . . .

from Tucson."

"Pleasure, ma'am. Otis Feltenmeyer, at your service," replied the corpulent colonel, bowing from the waist with an old-fashioned gallantry, this effort expelling an audible grunt as he came back to the vertical, perspiring and purple. "Permit me," he wheezed, and struck off into the glare of the post's parade, the girl in her ridiculous hat and whore's clothing scrambling along in his wake like a stray pup.

Pitiful! he thought. *Just plain, downright pitiful!*

"Commissary," he presently called gruffly, pointing out the sights. "Those buildings off there are barracks — enlisted men's quarters — out of bounds for ladies. Yonder is the dispensary, and those buildings you see at the far end are stables. This is Headquarters — the paperwork dungeon, and that group along there is called Officers' Row." He hauled up to look around at her. "Have you ever been on a post before?"

The girl, big-eyed, shook her mane of black hair.

Feltenmeyer gloweringly scrubbed at his jaw. "You'll be safe enough here. I must warn you, however, to stay inside the gates. The redskins are relatively quiet right now — can't cook up much mischief without

24

grass for their ponies. In a lot of ways this drought is a blessing. I'll be just as well pleased if the rains never come. There — this next house is mine."

A faded, motherly looking woman in gingham smiled from the open door of the porch.

"My dear," the colonel said, "this is Carmella Ramirez . . . from Tucson. She's come out here to marry that scamp, Barney Olds, and I've told her she can stay here with us for the moment. . . ."

Some three hours later, refreshed by a nap and some hasty ablutions, Carmella — fed to the gills with the strain of small talk and the evasion of questions she was not prepared to answer — left the house with a sigh of relief, glad to have the excuse of the good lady's suggestion that she step out and watch the flag lowering ceremony.

Her offer to help with the supper preparations had been thankfully refused and the cavalry companies had already left the stables when the girl softly closed the porch screen behind her.

The sun was just dropping behind the choppy march of humpbacked hills and the barked commands of by-the-book officers held the cadence of rote as horsemen wheeling smartly into line raised tiny explosions of dust from the packed caleche of the post's parade. Moving along the board walk she watched the companies assume regimental front, each mounted on horses uniformly matched in color, each flag rippling proudly in the lifted breeze from the tilted pole booted in the stirrup socket of the guidon corporal's footrest.

She could not help but experience some measure of pride in the sight of that long double rank of blue-clad shapes and stiffened faces all facing the company commanders and their adjutants, noting the first sergeants' reports as roll calls echoed up and down the rigid lines. It was a splendid sight, wondrously inspiring until one remembered the preposterous inadequacy of their spread-thin numbers against the vastness of the country.

Out by the flagpole as the companies were dismissed, the officers, having turned over their mounts, were idling along the far walk toward their quarters.

She reckoned, if Olds failed to show before her welcome wore thin, she could rope one of them and find security of sorts — better anyway than she was like to corral in Tucson, certain to be an improvement over the White Horse Bar which even now could set her teeth on edge.

But it was Olds she'd set her sights for. She wasn't about to take up with anyone else so long as there was any possibility of bagging him. Olds was a *hero,* the most lauded man to climb San Juan Hill, and everybody knew it no matter what they said now.

But more important even than this was Carmella's closely-clutched conviction that, back of all the lies and prodigal waste of time and substance, Olds held the key to the secrets of Yuma's chimney — that he'd been waiting only to get Lucky George off his back to grab that gold and clear out of the country. And when Barney left she was determined to be with him!

Engrossed in this and the problems it posed, she passed Headquarters and was approaching the guardbox held aloft on its tower, when the bray of a burro swung her face toward the gate.

It had not yet been closed and in the thickening shadows, figures half lost against the shapes of their horses, she glimpsed two men, the wheel of her glance picking out their hats and as swiftly forgetting them in the quickening interest awakened by the burro, the pick handle and shovel that protruded from its pack.

Was there ever another like it? she wondered, suddenly sure this was E. Pammynondas, a critter nearly as famous as its notorious owner, the indefatigable Barney.

Her heart thumped against her ribs like a drumbeat and she was painfully breathless, caught up in the portent and consequences of his coming. She wanted to run but her feet wouldn't move, frozen in their tracks by the realized brashness of all she had done and planned toward this moment.

One of the pair she had seen stepped out of the gate-side shadows and her eyes fiercely sharpened as she made recognition of that sly, too handsome face in its chin-strapped sombrero with the day's last light thinly winking from the crossed cartridge belts that heavily circled the snakelike hips.

Too well she recalled that cruel leer. This was the smuggler, Peep Goyanno, most valued customer of her late employer and still at large mainly because the border authorities thus far had failed to nab him with the goods. He was the kind that couldn't take no for an answer. Imagining himself to be irresistible it had been his pinchings and pawings which had driven her finally to get out of the place. It touched off cold shivers to discover him here so shortly after her own arrival and drawing back, disconcerted, she wondered if the fellow had deliberately followed her.

As though aware of her turmoil the man advanced, catlike of tread as some huge grinning spider, the mockery of his stare striking into her like needles.

"And did you think, my foolish one, Peep would not find you?"

Scarcely able to breathe she stood stiff in her tracks as a paralyzed rabbit, throat too parched to let go of a sound. Beyond the smuggler the odd loom of a limping man took shape between the posts of the gate and Carmella, revitalized, sprang beneath the startled spread of Goyanno's arms to fling herself, panting, against the newcomer's chest. "Barney — *Barney*," she sobbed — "I thought you'd *never* come!"

III

It had been some while since Barney Olds had found himself with a girl round his neck and, despite his considerable astonishment, he was not too distraught or too damned old to clamp his good arm about her. He'd been whacked so long by the winds of adversity he had learned to make the most of whatever Good Luck was careless enough to toss within reach.

In the rush of her embrace — with her hard up against him and this poor light and all, details tended to be a little fuzzy. He hadn't got much of a look at her but she sure as hell made him feel like a man; so when a whispery voice snarled out of the gloom, *"Get away from her, fool!"* Barney, grinning, only tightened his grip.

Metal glinted in the dusk and with a berserk fury the fellow flung himself at Olds. The prospector wasn't caught napping. Twenty-seven years of catch-as-catch can living had sharpened his perception of the laws of survival and bred in him a fine contempt for rules and conventions which ran contrary to nature. Still hanging onto Carmella, still grinning, he fetched up his left leg stiffly in the last possible moment and let the snarling man run into it.

A cry burst out of him as he staggered back. Olds went down, taking the girl with him, seeing a second crouched shape coming out of the shadows as, rolling, he got clear of her and scrambled to his feet. "Come on!" he growled, whipping the gun from his belt, but the second man fled in a rattle of hoofs as someone yelled from the tower: "Corporal of the Guard! Post Number One!"

The man Olds had kicked was still

doubled over, wheezing for breath, though he'd managed somehow to hang onto his knife. Olds, rushing forward, knocked it out of his grasp with a clout from his six-shooter and straightened him up with the lift of a knee. The fellow's eyes bulged, unfocused, and while he hung, frozen, half out on his feet, Barney drove a fist at his jaw. The fellow collapsed like a poleaxed beef.

The next thing Olds knew someone had jumped on his back and with an arm around his throat was trying to shut off his wind. Two other blurred shapes were lunging in from either side. Olds, fighting for breath, wheeled around in a circle, the flying heels of the man on his back cutting the other two down like the sweep of a scythe. There were yells and curses, the scuffle of boots, and then his vision dissolved in a burst of bright lights and he seemed to be sinking into a pool of black felt.

He came back, spluttering, gasping, the whole upper half of him drenched and still dripping, to find a trooper with an up-ended bucket standing over him.

"He's comin' round," someone said, and the trooper stepped aside while Olds got groggily up and felt himself over. "Guess I'm still among the quick," he grumbled at last. "What happened to my shootin' iron?"

A soldier handed it to him. Another held out his hat. "You must of been a red-striped sonofabitch before you lost that hand!" this fellow said; and then a sergeant came up to give him a jaundiced stare. "Colonel wants a few words with you, Olds. Better get over there on the double."

"Well, thanks for nothin'," Barney said, glowering, and still carrying his hat limped off toward headquarters, muttering under his breath.

Feltenmeyer, looking him over without favor, didn't bother to get up, push out the cigars or even ask him to sit down. "What's the matter," Barney said "— them damn bunions botherin' you again?"

"Never mind me." The Colonel spoke like his supper wasn't resting too good in him. "What have you got to say for yourself?"

Olds heaved a sigh. His head felt like a house had fallen on it. "I ain't found that gold, if that's what you're gettin' at."

The colonel's fishbelly stare never budged an inch.

"I guess it ain't," Barney growled, and looked around for a seat. He sighed again and said tentatively, "I could do with a drink if you've still got that bottle."

The old man said like he was dressing

down the troops: "I'm still waiting to hear your version of what happened out there, and — by God, sir, you're a disgrace to the Service!"

The culprit's wet shoulders slumped. He kind of shifted his weight in the once elegant boots that would have set back a ranch hand a good two months' pay and would never have come to their present condition on anyone but Olds. Made a man squirm just to look at them, so decrepit they were, weather-split and run over, the fancy sides so crisscrossed with scratches their original colors could only be guessed at.

"Yes, sir," answered Olds, sounding meek. But his lowered eyes and subdued tone of voice only further infuriated the exasperated colonel.

"Don't get smart with me!" he snapped. "For your own good, Olds, you ought to be locked up, and if I don't get a straight story . . ."

But there wasn't very much you could threaten him with, and both of them knew it. He wasn't subject to Army discipline now and there was no other kind Feltenmeyer could apply. He threw up his hands in frustration. "Get on with it!"

"First, I guess, you better know about Bloody Head — he's off the Reservation an' wearin' paint again. That bunch with him is ridin' cavalry mounts."

The colonel stared skeptically. "Bloody Head, eh? I find that hard to believe, though there's been some rumor of Fort Lowell losing . . . Just whereabouts did you —"

"I run into 'em first a bit south of Black Mountain. Knocked a couple of 'em sprawlin' but they camped on my trail till I got into that storm. If you want an opinion I'd say there's a fair t' middlin' chance they ain't five miles from where you're settin' right now."

Feltenmeyer, rubbing his jaw, looked thoughtful. "How many do you estimate there was in that bunch?"

"Not more'n a dozen, mebbe not over ten." Barney leaned forward. "If you was to send B Troop —"

The colonel said irritably: "I'll decide about that. Now suppose you run over that brawl at the gate." He slapped at a rumple of papers on his desk. "And I'd suggest you stick to the facts for a change."

Olds said with a shrug, "Where you want me to start?"

"Why not begin with that feller you jumped?"

The prospector scowled. "*I* never jumped anyone!"

34

They glared at each other. The colonel said skeptically, "Like always, the innocent bystander." His tone turned cold. "That feller's been questioned —"

"Never mind," Olds growled. "You asked for the truth an' that's what you're gettin'. I come through that gate — still feelin' to see did I have all my hair — an' some female actin' like it was her had been chased comes hellity larrup an' all but takes a strangle hold on me. Whilst I was fixin' to unlatch myself this Mex comes sloshin' up out of the shadders, lets out a squawk an' makes a pass with a knife. Now I ask you! What kinda fool would wait t' git himself skewered?"

"There's nothing in the report I have here about a knife."

"He had one," Olds said. "I knocked it out of his fist."

"And you never saw this feller before?"

"I never seen either of 'em — the girl *or* the guy. Not t' know it, anyway. Tell you the truth, now that I come t' think about it, I reckon it was *her* that Mex'kin was after."

"Don't push me, Olds." The colonel said like it pained him: "I am not entirely powerless in this matter. I can have you held for disorderly conduct, send for the civilian authorities and keep you incommunicado till they come and take you off my hands."

He eyed Barney more in pity than in anger. "Feller prowling that desert all the time like you've been is bound, I suppose, to come up with some pretty queer notions. No one around but a burro to talk to."

Barney's look of bewilderment brought a flush to the officer's cheeks. But the man's past record mitigated in his favor and the colonel said at last, "I imagine there are extenuating circumstances to which I'll give ear if you want to take me into your confidence; but I've put that jigger in the guardhouse, Olds, and a full report is going to have to be made of it. Think careful now. You want to change that story?"

"For Chris'sake, Colonel, I've *told* you the truth! What is this, anyway?"

Feltenmeyer sighed. "That Mexican says the girl was his woman, that you've been . . . ah, paying her attentions —"

"The guy's crazy as hell! What is he, some kinda nut?"

"You can't deny she threw her arms around you, called you by name. It's right here in the corporal's report. That chap's an alleged smuggler — Peep Goyanno. Swears he'll kill you, Olds."

But Olds just continued to stare.

"All right," growled the colonel. "I gave

you credit for more gumption than that. If you've been cutting a rusty with a girl that isn't yet out of her teens, don't look to me to get you off the hook."

Olds was staring open-mouthed. In the lamp bracketed over the colonel's desk he appeared a deal paler than when he'd come in. By Gad, it was nauseous to see Olds wasted on trumpery of this sort, stooping to use a girl in such fashion — and a poor defenseless orphan at that. Distastefully Feltenmeyer said with a scowl, "This child came in on the noon stage from Tucson, expecting you to meet her —"

"Hell's fire," Olds snarled, "I never seen her before!"

"You don't have to shout, and I'll tell you right now that doesn't gee with the facts. She claims you two were engaged to be married — 'betrothed' was the word she used, I believe. Man, it just won't wash! She recognized you on sight, called you by name. According to what the corporal's got down here," he growled, fingering his papers, "she . . . here it is — 'ran to Olds, flinging both arms around his neck, sobbing and calling him twice by name. He hugged her, too.' You can't get around that."

"But —"

"Now hear this. I'll give you till exactly

seven in the morning to set matters straight or make a clean breast of it." The colonel pushed back his chair. "I don't care to get into the intimacies of it, but if I'm not satisfied in the morning about this I'm holding you over with Goyanno for the sheriff. She'll likely prefer charges. And that's all I have to say to you."

IV

Like Barney said to himself as he was quitting Headquarters, that Mex and his threats had nothing to do with the high price of bacon. Feltenmeyer was the big gun here, and he'd meant every word of that ultimatum.

Any attempt at escape could powerful easy get a man shot, but the penalties for staying were infinitely more frightening. In country like this that fool girl's lies could leave him kicking at the end of a rope. All the cards were against him, all the mooching and dodges, the hoaxes he'd launched to keep himself grubstaked — every belly laugh wrung from the pranks he'd indulged in. He could shout himself hoarse and who would believe him?

Nope. He had to clear out and the sooner the better.

Be no great trick to slip over the wall but getting a burro out by this route was pretty obviously impossible, and he sure didn't want to leave E. Pammynondas. Old Pammy over the years had become his man Friday, companion, watchdog, and beast of burden — the most dependable partner a man ever had. And, as of right now, he didn't even know where the burro was!

Probably, he reckoned, somewhere around the stables. A real forager, was Pammy, with a fine nose for tasties and a colossal contempt for the rights of private property. Regardless of what these yellowlegs thought of Olds and his didos, none of this bunch would be so hardhearted as to leave a hungry animal uncared for, he guessed.

But a hurried check of the stable area failed to provide any clue to Pammy's whereabouts, nor had any of the troopers he questioned admitted to having seen the animal. Puzzled, worried and about to give up, Barney finally called out to one of the sentries up on the rampart, asking only if the man had seen a burro wandering about.

"I seen some kinda jackass over toward Post Number One a while ago."

Barney peered in that direction. "Was the gate still open?"

"Seems t' me it was," the guard said and,

shouldering his rifle, set off to meet his opposite number.

Olds stared and peered and still wasn't sure, though, with full dark hardly minutes away, it seemed mighty likely the gate was closed now. And of course it might not have been Pammy anyway. There were mules on this post. That guy on the ramp might have seen one of them, which had somehow got loose . . . but if that were so why hadn't he reported it?

Why, indeed? They'd been swift enough to report *him,* drat 'em!

He scowled at the windows of the sutler's bar, lamplit squares of butter yellow against the deepened dark of a soot-colored night. He was minded, by grab, to go tie one on, and likely would have if he hadn't been stony. Seemed like a million stars were out and, as Olds peered about with sharpening glance, it came over him there were too many lights winking and flittering all of a sudden.

His brows drew down in a disquieting frown. Prickling chills like a patter of fingers tiptoed down his spine as he stared. "Lanterns!" he growled on a shiver of breath. Like a gathering of fireflies they moved through the stables and, off to the other side, appeared to be thickening about the main gate.

With a muttered curse Olds came out of his trance. The wink and shift of those lanterns meant a search was in progress and the stepped-up pound of his pulse assured him there could only be one answer to that. Obviously orders had gone out to make sure a certain prospector was going to be around for that seven o'clock meeting with the colonel tomorrow!

Agitation raced through Olds like a brush fire. No question of his getting a fair hearing; he hadn't a Chinaman's chance with the lies of that blabbermouthed girl stacked against him! Without scanning this further he backed into the deeper black of spiked poles, teeth bared in the snarl of a cornered lynx.

El Mocho, they called him down here on the border. Well, he might be one-handed but there was nothing the matter with his sense of survival. Crouched there in the dark, his whole future unfolded in a two-legged series of panic-spooked pictures — himself in double harness and himself at the end of some hangman's damned rope.

Self preservation was the first law of nature. Burro forgotten, he went over the wall.

41

He dropped with a thud and hung there, heart pounding, hand against the peeled poles of the stockade. For what seemed an eternity he squatted, frozen in his tracks, before he dared pull a fresh breath into him. And even then he did not move, so sure had he been that a cry would go up.

But nothing happened, no alarm was sounded. In patched and brush-clawed blue denim and the red flannel shirt that had been sun faded to the likeness of strawberry pink, he finally straightened, to probe the surrounding dark.

He picked up his bearings, but now where to go? They couldn't do much about finding him tonight but with first light they'd have trackers and at least one patrol casting around for him — pretty near bound to, he thought, fingering his belt to make sure his six-shooter hadn't come loose. Alone, afoot, they'd expect him to make for some ranch or town where he could find transportation to get him out of the country. He had a vision of reward dodgers plastered all over, and swore in a fury of fear and trepidation.

He'd fool them, by grab, lose himself in the furnace winds and burning sands of the desert. He knew places, by God, not even Indians had been — but he sure as hell wished he had E. Pammynondas. With his trusty burro he could have out-foxed them sure!

He pulled in his belt, knowing the need to cover ground before the broil of another sun got high enough over this empty waste to force him into lying doggo. Through a clamor of places spinning through his head he had to sort out the best deal he could get, some refuge he might reach soon enough to get under cover before he was spotted. He was already moving in the direction of the river when a sibilant *"Psssst!"* leached eerily through the whirl of his thoughts.

Olds stopped like he'd run into a rock, the inside of his mouth suddenly dry as pouched powder. Strive as he would he couldn't make out a thing in this coagulated gloom. Shadows hemmed him like a smother of blankets. He couldn't pick out the faintest flicker of motion. It was like he was standing in a sea of blue ink.

It could have been a snake, and he was beginning to wonder if he'd imagined the sound when a disembodied whisper floated out of the dark. "Over here," it called. "I've got your burro. We're in the mesquites."

Barney's head stiffly swung to scan the murk off to the right but found no brush that he could make out. He peered left then, presently discerning what appeared to be a thickening of shadows possibly fifty feet away, on a line with the wash he'd come up to reach the post.

It crossed his mind this might easily be some kind of trap rigged to put him in reach of a knife or a gunstock, but possession of that burro could make all the difference between whether he got clear or wound up feeding a flock of dang buzzards. With a cold ball rolling up inside his gut he palmed his pistol and moved warily ahead.

Never in his wildest imaginings would he have expected to encounter what awaited him. Drawing nearer the heavier gloom of the thicket the feeling of peril increased. Through the thorn-spiked branches he spotted the long ears and sad face of Pammynondas, but the relief this brought was swiftly lost in the glimpse Olds caught of the burro's companion.

The hair on his neck rose up like hackles. There wasn't much he could see but the trap smell suddenly was all around, queerly stirred by some indefinable memory which fetched him, peering, to an uncertain halt.

"I've filled your cantina — hadn't we better be moving?"

Olds, skin crawling, didn't want to believe it but the voice, no longer whispering, confirmed his bitterest fears. Pammy's two-legged friend was the ornery witch that had got him into this bind in the first place — the girl who'd embraced him as he came through the gate.

V

"We're not goin' no place!" he growled, striding forward, angrily reaching for the burro's rope.

But her hand was there first and he snatched back his fist as though he'd struck hot iron.

The stars, seeming now scarce a rope's toss away, gave down plenty of light to make out, this close up, the cool mockery on her face. "Were you afraid it was Goyanno? He'll be after us, you know — mud and bars will never hold him."

"Not after *us*," Barney snarled, "because you're not goin'! You better git that through your cabeza right now!"

A pretty tinkle of sound came through the shine of her teeth and that confident look grew even more brazen as she said imper-turbably, "You want me to scream and bring

45

the post down on you?"

Barney licked cracked lips and she murmured, still amused, "That commandant is such a self-righteous John — can't you just see his face when they discover you've abducted me?"

Olds could, indeed. He found himself sweating and swallowed convulsively, almost whining as he cried: "You don't know what it's like out there on that desert — hot enough, dang it, t' fry a gal's eyeballs! Tops a hundred an' twenty in the shade an' there ain't none. You loco or somethin'?"

She smiled at him sweetly. "We're just wasting good time. You can't scare me. I've heard every yarn they tell about you and nothing you can say is going to change my mind. When you quit this post I'm quitting it with you."

"You musta lost your marbles," he growled, and reached again for the rope.

She held it away from him, smiling but defiant.

Olds clenched his fist, looking minded to hit her. "Go ahead," she said, pushing her jaw out. "Knock me silly. Beat me insensible if that's the way you want them to find me."

Olds dropped his arm. Groaning he said, "Get off my back, will you?"

She shook her black mane, and very

becoming it was, too. "You're stuck with me, Olds. You might as well get used to it."

"You're worse'n a gadfly," Barney snarled. But she certainly had him. He could strike off and leave her but he sure couldn't stop the little fool from following, not without deliberately setting out to lose her — they'd hunt him down with dogs if he tried anything like that. He swore disgustedly.

She was the pushiest female he had ever run into. A bundle of contradictions, and hardly no bigger'n a golrammed minute. Yet even in the clutch of Olds' frustrations he was not unmindful of her flamelike grace or the big-eyed way she had of staring back at him. And he could still remember the feel of her against him. . . .

But she was right about one thing. All the proof he needed was in the sudden wink of lanterns bobbing off yonder amongst the scurry of figures milling antlike in the maw of that reopened gate. If he was minded to get clear he had better get a move on.

He peered round at her again, harried by time and the complications her unwanted presence thrust so bitterly upon him. "What about your folks? It don't make sense you traipsin' off into a goddam desert with a one-armed jigger that ain't got two nickels he could rub together. Be reasonable, girl!

You ain't got the strength fer it!"

"Try me," she said.

Barney rolled his eyes. "I ain't scarcely got enough grub fer myself — you'd have t' walk every inch of it! Feel that wind? Feel the sting of it — that's grit! Sand's liftin' again, an' we're short on water. No one but a total fool would head into that with no more reason than *you* got!"

She threw a look toward the post. "Won't be nobody going if you don't get started."

Barney knew when he was beat. Without another word he took off down the wash like a wet-footed cat.

She held up a lot better than he would ever have imagined, never once complaining, even vehemently protesting when in the cold cheerless time just before the false dawn he stripped the pack from old Pammy and ordered her up. When, jaw slack from fatigue and looking ready to drop, she was too pooped even to protest anymore, Olds unceremoniously scooped her up and plopped her down on the burro's back. "Now set there," he growled, "an' don't give me no sass!"

He'd been pretty near finished himself, truth to tell, when a couple hours back he'd turned loose of the lead shank and thrown down the pack in a shallow draw thinly screened by dwarf cedar high up on the flank of a windy mountain. He had lifted her down half asleep like she was, put both his blankets over her, given Pammy a drink, and gone back into the cedars to have a look at their backtrail.

Clear and brisk as it was in these early hours with the sun peering over the Santa Teresas some sixty miles east, he figured to spot anything that showed motion. But he looked a good while before he finally did, and then it was on the road south toward Mammoth, a slow moving dust likely kicked up by horses that brought a saturnine grin from Olds as he put down his glass. They could comb that country till hell froze over for all the difference it made to him.

He sat there a while, too weary to get up, his mind on the girl and the problems she presented, trying to dredge up some way of ridding himself of her. He'd have been all right and deep into the desert except for that storm and having to hold down his pace to accommodate this clabber-headed frail. What in Tophet was she up to? Why was she so bound and determined to go skallyhootin' off into the brush with him?

Sure beat the cars the kind of fool notions women latched on to anymore. What was it old Feltenmeyer had said, that according to

her, him and her was betrothed? And yesterday the first time he'd ever clapped eyes on
her!

Girl that fetching would pretty near have
to have *some* pins missing to bed down with
anything balmy as that. A looker, too — and
him with one flipper! Not to mention the
years he had put down the drain before ever
they'd spanked her to open her eyes.

Might as well hope to scratch your neck
with your elbow as try to find logic in a
female mind.

But one thing showed as plain as plowed
ground. Unless he was fixing to slip into
double harness he'd do well to cut loose of
her at soonest opportunity. With them
whoppers she'd told — and the both of
them missing — a man in his boots could
inherit real trouble.

If only she wasn't so gawd-awful young!

VI

Morosely chewing at his lip, Olds took up
his glass, moving it over that barren view,
quartering the duns and lemon yellows,
those chalky reds and rusty browns that lay
tossed up like a frozen sea, with Camp
Grant hidden behind the hulk of Lookout
Mountain, almost black where it reared

across the climbing slant of the sun.

They'd come perhaps twelve miles in their flight from the post, no great ways he was forced to admit, but at least that storm would have buried their tracks for a part of the distance — the earlier stretch.

He was pulling what rather wistful satisfaction he could from this and from that faint whirl of dust on the Mammoth road when, lowering his lens to sweep the middle distance, he went rock still, intent on something picked out of the far left, tiny antlike figures crawling over the sand, not hurrying enough to lift any dust but definitely moving, dead on his trail and irrevocably pointed straight at this mountain.

In the harassment of nearer problems he'd forgot all about Bloody Head and his Apaches. It didn't look, however, like they had forgot *him.*

Collapsing his glass he thrust it under the stump of his handless arm, got down off his rock and, scowling bitterly, cut back toward Pammy and the still sleeping girl.

This was not a good place to try and stand off Apaches. Too easy got at and a sight too open for a man that set any value on his hair. They were still, anyways, six to seven miles off, so there was no sense bothering the girl just yet. Better to let her rest while she could. They'd have a hard push in front of them once they dropped off the side of this mountain.

Off and on through a stretch of barren months too long to keep track of, Bloody Head's bunch of bronco Apaches had been camped on his trail, and every so often this worrisome persistence would erupt into a murderous trading of hostilities. Up to this point Barney had been terribly lucky, the result very possibly of unremitting vigilance. But now, preoccupied with complications thrust upon him by the girl and his dwindling supplies, the immediate future did not look rosy. Put bluntly, that future looked disquietingly unlikely.

Once he'd got off the desert he'd taken some pains to bollix up the trail but he wasn't unduly heartened by this. Those dang Injuns were experts at reading sign and the most he could hope for was to have gained a little time, perhaps enough to lay a false trail if he got right at it, and wasn't spotted doing it. There might be a bare chance if he left the girl here that he could lead them away from her, but it looked pretty bare.

Tracks already seen would have told the Apaches that during the night there'd been two of them, that the lighter sign had been left by a female or boy. If Olds' tracks quit here alone them ornery buggers was a heap more likely — even if they saw him — to split up, and even if Barney managed to get clear he would have to live with what happened to that girl hung round his neck for the rest of his days.

He was roused from this lugubrious prospect by the girl's sharp exclamation of dismay. She had suddenly pushed up and, not seeing him behind her, assumed he'd taken off. She got loose of the blankets and, scrambling to her feet, peered around pretty wildlike. With her hair every whichway she was a sight — kind of pitiful, too, if a feller could forget the kind of drag she put on him.

But what a change when she saw him! The whole scared look of her brightened up, and then as swiftly darkened with distrust and reproach when she discovered the pistol still gripped in his hand.

Barney grinned at her sourly. "We better git movin'."

Belting the six-shooter he picked up the blankets and whistled for Pammy. The burro waggled one ear but kept on with the business of translating some brush ends into the make-do of breakfast.

Rummaging two blackened lumps of

unsavory looking jerky from the pack, Barney handed her one. "Better git some of that under yer belt," he said, and growled at the burro. "Chris'sake, Pammy! We ain't got all day — git over here, dang you!" He glanced around at the girl. "What in Tophet do they call you?"

"Carmella." She still seemed to be having a bit of trouble with her breathing, though she managed with obvious effort to unfurl the flutter of a trepidant smile. "Carmella Ramirez . . . at your orders," she added timidly as the burro reluctantly edged up to Olds.

Barney, scowling, stowed the blankets and somewhat dubiously got Pammy ready. He appeared to be in two minds about something but did not take her into his confidence. He eyed her a moment, then let go of his wind with an ill-concealed snort. "Let's go," he grumbled and, scooping up the halter shank, struck off up the draw without bothering to look back.

Where the dry watercourse played out against the flaked-off rock at the foot of a cliff, a tiny deer trail angled through the brush on a downward trend Olds hoped might eventually put them back on the flats, while serving to hide their movements from the Indians.

One thing you could bet your bottom dollar on. This wasn't going to be more than a temporary respite; he saw no chance of piling up enough leeway to keep out of sight for more than a few hours. There were not any holes out there on the desert they could manage to get into short of nightfall.

"You speak pretty good for a Mex," he called back as they turned into this trail. But she made no reply and presently, a little uneasy, he twisted a backward look, but she was coming, pinched of cheek, trudging along in his wake a good piece back.

Standing by Pammy he pulled up, scowling, to wait, their four-footed friend making use of this pause to continue his sampling of nearby branches. Considering moodily the on-coming girl, who certainly wasn't pushing herself any, he reckoned his cup was filled to overflowing.

With that face of an angel he found the things she'd told Feltenmeyer — if she really *had* told them — powerful hard to figure. Yet why would the colonel have lied to him about it? He guessed you had to accept them, unlikely or not. But *why?* that's what puckered him. Why would she want to claim a thing like that? He not only wasn't handsome, he wasn't even a whole man! Why, he was dang near old enough to be the girl's father — too dang near! he thought with a grimace.

When she was close enough to hear without making a project of it, Olds gruffly said: "There's six-eight Injuns camped on our sign. If you don't want to join 'em you better keep up."

She gave him a sharp look but did not clobber him with questions. He guessed she thought he was pulling her leg, but she did move a mite more spry when Olds, hauling the reluctant burro away from his lunch, again set off down the trail.

She was a cool one, though. A feller ought to give the devil his due. Most frails, flogged with the threat of Apaches, would of gone plumb into the screaming willies, or made out to, anyhow. Hooped and dried, that black mop of hers would make some buck a prime decoration, and the prospect stirred Barney into some rather unlikely and seldom prowled avenues of thought before he took hold of himself with a snort and choused his attention back to the urgencies of survival.

It depended on how much time he could pile up. And to gain that time he'd have to — about mid morning or thereabouts — put on a show of panicked flight *and sustain it until dark.*

To make this palatable to suspiciously watching redskins a man would have to go tearing with reckless haste into the most abandoned and waterless hellhole imaginable within reach of these sunblasted flats — the dreaded Valle del Cráneo, the valley of skulls. Only by a display of rushing headlong and unwittingly into what had been for a lot of damn fools an inescapable deathtrap might these Apaches allow him the time he so frantically needed if he was to elude them.

VII

Following Barney and his cinnamon burro, Carmella found doubts of her own to contend with. Back in Tucson *anything* had looked better than the hateful indignities she'd been forced to put up with in the hectic life of the White Horse Bar. Now she wasn't so sure. Running off with the hero of San Juan Hill had seemed a glorious adventure, richly frosted with the dazzle of profits . . . but how shabbily the facts were falling short of the promise.

And the man himself!

Not only — surprisingly — was Olds unappreciative, he was downright boorish — even, apparently, *resentful*. Instead of a slave she'd dug up a slave driver!

It was astonishing, bewildering, and beginning to upset her. Well, who wouldn't be disturbed! What was the matter with him? You would think he hadn't any blood in his veins! How could you bargain with a man who wasn't interested?

So maybe he wasn't the marrying kind — but that wouldn't account for the way he'd been treating her. Not even at the White Horse had anyone been so purely aggravating — exasperating, yes, but there had been no lack of interest. She'd been *somebody* there, provocative and wanted, while from the start of their acquaintance, Olds had scarcely been civil.

Now he thought to scare her off with Indians!

If she hadn't been so furious she would have laughed in his face at such preposterous talk. The Indians had all been cooped up long ago and everybody knew it — why, she'd actually felt sorry for their plight, such a comedown it was from their once proud position. It was humiliating to be reminded he considered her such a goose.

She got to thinking back over things she'd heard and oddly enough, now her mind was on it, could not seem to connect him up with anything having to do with a woman.

Frustration pushed her chin out and the needs she felt turned the red lips thin as she angrily eyed the burly shoulders of this man whose determined search for a hidden chimney of gold seemed the likeliest means she might find in this world to rise above the things she had come from.

He would find she could be as determined as he was! She wasn't about to give up and turn back — not with empty hands, anyway. He may have stepped around women in the past but he wasn't going to step around her! He might treat her like excess baggage right now, but he had met his match in Carmella Ramirez, and she would see that he knew it if it was the last thing she did!

But as the morning wore on and they dropped down into the building heat of the flats it became increasingly hard even to maintain a semblance of keeping up. She couldn't think what had got into the man.

As the sun climbed higher into the glare of sky she had almost to run merely to stay even. More and more often she fell behind. Weird pictures took shape against the blank of her brain. Her throat grew dry as a fire under stove lids, each breath a burning agony.

She tried to cry out, to call ahead to him to wait, to let her rest or at least catch up, but all that came out were tiny buzzardlike croaks, so horribly faint she scarcely heard them herself.

Even the horizon entered into the conspiracy, wavering, tilting crazily, first to one side, then to the other. Sand and sky appeared to blend and writhe until up and down no longer had any meaning. At times she seemed almost to be floating in a cocoon of light curling round her like a flame. There were times she even thought to smell the scorch of flesh, but someway she managed to keep staggering on, reeling and floundering like a *paisano borracho.*

She didn't know Olds had stopped until blindly she ran into him. Recoiling in shock, she would almost certainly have fallen had that quick right arm not caught and closed around her. Numb with relief, she collapsed against him, too beat even to whimper.

The next thing she knew was the feel of wet cloth on her face and a ridge of arm supporting her half-raised shoulders, the feel of hot sand against the backs of legs and hips. Even through the thin folds of her skirts she could feel its ferocious heat, and she struggled to get away from it, moaning, gasping as the slap of Olds' hands stung tingling cheeks and rocked her head.

She tore herself away from him, scrambling furiously up to sway dizzily a moment until things swam into recognizable focus. She glared at him then, lips drawn back like an angry tigress. "Try that again and I'll cut your heart out!"

The man's gray eyes, half shut in the brightness, widened a little and turned whimsically speculative. "Mebbe you would at that," he conceded "— or anyway try." He peered over his shoulder and, twisting back, considered her again. "We better git crackin'."

Filled with outrage, she cried: "You might at least give me time to catch my breath!"

His eyes turned dark. "You've had twenty minutes. That's all we kin spare."

He went over to the burro, not waiting for an argument, and came back to thrust the water bag at her. "Slosh some around in your mouth but don't drink more'n a coupla swallers."

She unstoppered the bag and put the rim to her mouth. But when, ignoring him, she threw back her head to let that heavenly coolness run down her throat, Olds snatched the bag away. "You tryin' t' make yourself sick? If you're goin' with me, you'll do like I tell you, when an' *ever' damn time* I tell you! Savvy?"

Peering into the scowl of that flintlike stare

Carmella's mouth became two white rims. With a flash of teeth she turned loose some of her own fiery temper. "Go!" she cried fiercely "— go on if you're scared! Don't worry about *me!*"

She hadn't meant that, of course, but it was quickly apparent he intended taking it for gospel. Revealing no intention of worrying about her he put his left shoulder into the water bag's strap, unsnapped the lead shank from Pammy's halter and, swinging it, choused the reluctant burro off ahead of him into the curls and writhings of heat that wriggled like the ghosts of dead snakes above that bright blaze of sand.

She hung back with mixed emotions, half convinced he would quit when this stage-managed threat got no change out of her. Then, staring appalled when he kept right on going — never once twisting round — she broke into an alarmed run.

But the sand was too loose. She couldn't keep it up. Sweat cracked through the pores of her flesh and inside twenty strides she was reduced once again to the groggy foot-frying walk she'd been in half the morning. Too dog beat to more than occasionally lift her head in a trancelike stare, she plodded endlessly on, dropping farther behind, numbly pulling one lead-weighted foot after the other from the voracious, never-ending suck of fiery sand.

She lost track of time, presently losing sight even of Olds himself, to go wallowing on through that nightmare of heat, a blind horse on a treadmill, unthinking, half fried in the terrible furnace breath of this inferno, lurching and staggering through the burning glare, less and less conscious of the tracks that were the sole reality and proof he was still somewhere up there in front of her.

Someplace in the searing grip of those hours she tore off the swaddling bundle of petticoats, abandoning them one after the other till only the loose-swinging folds of her skirt brushed against the scalded touch of chafed legs.

Somewhere too, during that time, she grew obsessed with the notion of unseen eyes spying out her every motion, watching, waiting with a malice she could feel and which, finally, drove her into prodigally pouring the last dregs of her strength into trying once more to overhaul the vanished Olds.

She became too light-headed, too fried dry of moisture, to presently know what she was doing. The last thing she did with any coherent semblance of reality was to get the chin up off her burning chest for a despairing red-eyed look roundabout and it was then, peering painfully, that she finally found herself lost in the immensity of rust-colored rocks and blinding sand that stretched everywhere unbroken toward each desolate horizon.

There were no tracks to follow. She was utterly alone.

VIII

Olds had all but forgotten her in his preoccupation with plans for outfoxing those bronco Apaches. It was the down-slanting flight of a spiraling shadow which first dragged his thoughts grimly back to the girl. Scowling up he shook a scornful fist at the birds, and then his stare drew down in surprised perplexity when, glancing over his shoulder, he first discovered she wasn't still back of him.

Inclined to doubt his own eyes he got the glass from his pack, convinced she was briefly lost in some trough of the innumerable ridges of sand. But when, after five minutes of testily scanning, he still failed to pick up a flutter of movement, Olds bitterly cursed.

He had just come in sight of the goal he'd

been aiming for, the sheer rock portals which, towering off yonder, opened into the forbidding Valley of Skulls, and he was loath to go back on any time-wasting hunt that would put those devils any nearer than they already were. He hadn't any doubt they were hot on his trail or watching from some rise, waiting only for him to lock himself into this trap which had closed on so many of his unfortunate contemporaries.

But Olds — still alive — wasn't walking into this blind. He knew considerable about that waterless box canyon that had but one way in and no other way out.

More than just a few times in those long winter months before Bloody Head had sworn to catch and roast him, Barney had camped in it with Pammy, had prospected the place — even found some traces of color in addition to the bright vermillion reds of its ghoulish sandstone cliffs; had foreseen the possibility of sometime being run into it by enemies and had taken steps accordingly. He had never imagined such an embarrassing occurrence as this present situation, but had laid in the means — including buried water — of withstanding anything likely to be thrown at him.

Which were dang good arguments against the obvious hazards of turning back now, but there wasn't any help for it. He might not be in line for any harp or halo but there were some kinds of things a feller couldn't stomach and go on calling himself a man.

No matter what she'd done, or whose fault it was, he sure couldn't leave that fool girl out there to die of thirst or Injun attrocities.

Still mumbling and muttering, he thought old Pammy in reasonably good shape and, bitterly cursing, got him turned around. Hoping against all sensible conclusions they wouldn't have to go far, he put the lead shank back on the burro's halter and set off, scowling, to retrace ground already counted covered.

No one had to point out to Olds the mighty grim dangers in going back after her; it was cutting the odds pretty fine, and he knew it. He should have looked round more often — it was plain enough now. But ingrained habits were powerful hard to break and, to this point anyway, he'd never had to think of anyone but himself. And, of course, Pammy.

The air of this place was stifling by now, the cooked-out quality of it was like breathing flame, but what plagued Olds even more than this, peering ahead against that brassy glare, was this worrisome inability to discover or turn up the faintest indication that those dang savages were still after him. It wasn't like Injuns — broncos in particular — to be lally-gaggin around this way. Even if they figured to have him boxed, there ought to be signs of *some* activity.

It was the loneliest landscape a man would want to look at. Not a peak showed smoke. Not a mirror flash winked in all that broiling spread-out hell of desolation. Nothing moved anywhere but Olds and his burro, and he was getting damned tired of hauling on that bastardly rope when he finally found where the girl had turned off.

Glowering at those pitiful tracks, it almost seemed she'd tried, he thought, to hit up a run; and he covertly peered uneasily about. It was the why of this that gnawed him worst. Had this sudden spurt been the piled-up result of sheer desperation, or had something given her cause for real fright?

He reckoned a wide enough circle might provide some answers — at least indications — but he'd neither the time nor energy for this. He could see that Pammy didn't like it, either, the way he was snuffling — setting back, by grab, like a mule in a hailstorm! Olds finally had to take the rope to the bastard in order to make him move out on her tracks.

It was a worrying business trying to search

for the girl while keeping one eye skinned out for an ambush; and the deteriorating look of what sign she had left was not calculated to much improve a man's prospects.

Fortunately he did not have to go far — scarcely a hundred paces beyond their trail, and there she was, sprawled face down like an abandoned rag doll. Olds felt his stomach turn over inside him.

White as a gutted snowbird, pinched of cheek and cracked of lip — still, by God, as the rock of ages! But bad as she looked he found, when he caught up with conflicting emotions, she was at least still breathing, and he gave thanks for that . . . though it later occurred to him to wonder why.

He got her onto the burro, after removing the pack, with a deal of cursing to make the snorting beast hold still for it. Chafed her wrists and wet her face, heard a couple of groans roll out of her mouth, but no sense came into the fixed wide-open eyes. It sure bugged him to think what to do.

It was while his own stare was quartering round that he chanced to look back and catch, across the hunch of one turning shoulder, the ragged banner of dust streaking toward him and the shapes joggling through it, the wicked glinting of rifles where the sun struck their lifted barrels.

He needed no instruction in what this meant. His hand seemed all thumbs but he got her tied on. She still looked a goner but he was damned if he would leave her; and there was one other chore he reckoned better be tended.

Where his tracks went around it he stripped leaves and twigs from a tall branch of greasewood, tore a hunk off his shirttail and tied it there in plain sight. In the language of the desert this was blunt warning, a deadly order to turn back or take the consequences. He didn't imagine it would stop them but they'd know he meant business and it might turn them cautious, give him time enough anyhow to get under cover.

They were still miles away, but not many. Not nearly enough for the ground he must regain. This could be a close thing — no use kidding himself. In this furnace-like heat, and the miles already covered, he hadn't a chance if he broke out of a walk — he wouldn't get no farther than this fool girl had got, and grimly knew it.

Grabbing up the pack, estimating the distance yet to be covered to put them between those rock portals off yonder, he discarded his pick with a growl of regret — even, finally, throwing down his shovel in the hope its weight might make the difference, hit the burro a lick and set off, fear like a lump wedged between his bowed shoulders.

Though he was bursting to hurry he made himself doggedly hold to his pace, trying to keep panic from making a fool of him. One wrong move at this stage of the game and those damned circling birds would sail down for a feast!

The next time he looked those breech-clouted devils were pulled up round his flag in a powwow-like huddle; and they were near enough now for him to pick out Bloody Head, squat and rocklike on the red-and-white pinto, where he sat hearing the gesticulated arguments Barney's shirttail had provoked.

It was suddenly apparent they were wasting their breath. The boss man viciously shoved his mount between them and, without so much as opening his mouth, took off on Olds' trail, the rest, regardless of personal preference, falling in behind.

They were scarcely more than a mile away and could certainly see El Mocho brandishing his rifle, but no one turned back.

With a curse Barney cuffed the burro into motion.

IX

With barely a quarter of a mile yet to go it became brutally apparent Olds wasn't going to make it — not, leastways, this side of gunfire. The narrow slitlike entrance between those red rock bastions, though plain to see, might as well have been at the far end of China for all the good it would do him right now with those howling red devils practically nipping at his heels.

Flinging down his pack Barney snatched free his rifle. Running up to the burro which had stopped to peer back at him Olds, fiercely shouting, gave him a resounding thump across the rump with the butt of it. But that bewildered old friend, eyes reproachfully rolling, stood fast in his tracks, never budging an inch. The girl still was unconscious.

"Git goin', you dang knucklehead!" Barney yelled, waving his arms. "Go on — *git her outa this!*"

Pammy pawed at the ground and blew through his nose.

Olds, damply frantic, saw that halfway measures were like to get them both killed. Reversing his Henry furiously he drove a blue whistler between the burro's legs. Fired again.

A gout of cinnamon hair flew off Pammy's flank. With eyes wildly rolling he came unstuck. Snorting alarm he went straight into the air, whirled in mid-flight and came down hammering sand with all fours. Both ears flopping, he took off like the deer flies was after him. Olds put one more slug past his head and spun about to unlimber another into the staring huddle of motionless redskins.

They came apart, too, and Barney, dropping, sought the meager cover of his grounded pack. Bellied flat in the sand with the slugs thwacking round him he found time to wonder in a twinge of bitter irony why — with water, grub and cartridges cached to his need just behind the red rock mouth of that pocket — he had crazily toted the pack this far.

One lucky shot took the hat off his head. Another nipped at the heel of his boot while a third tugged the loose end of the red bandanna stuffed into a hip pocket. This was getting too warm for comfort and, scrinching himself into as small a target as possible, Barney slid the barrel of his cherished repeater across the bulge of his pack and, taking quick aim, turned loose a flight of hornets.

Two arm-waving Apaches went off their

horses like hell wouldn't have them; a third, swaying giddily, went larruping off. A horse went down wildly squealing, his erstwhile rider — catapulted into the clear — picking himself out of a spraddle to stagger up looking as though most of the brains had been shook out of him. As Olds wheeled his sights the rest of them fled out of range.

Barney shook his fist at them. "Thought you wanted a fight!" he yelled, and called them every dirty name he could think of.

But they'd be back, and back in a hurry if he looked like making ready to bolt. They were still out for blood, and preferably his. Though he hooted and jeered he wasn't doubting their courage. Apaches was the fiercest of all red-skinned fighters, crafty as Eve's serpent and if, as now, they weren't showing much stomach, it wasn't because their sand had run out. It was only that they liked a good edge and the loss of two braves and a bronc wasn't their idea of something to cheer about. Anyone daffy enough to figure different had a heap to learn about Injuns, Olds mused, and took the time to replace his spent cartridges.

It was a good thing, he thought, that his sixgun and rifle used the same ammunition, and dug all the spare rounds he had from his pack, placing a mound of them ready to his hand. After which he looked around, not much caring for his placement in this predicament.

There was too much open back of where he lay, plenty of room for an Apache circle, and precious little he could see to do about it. They had him cold and could take their time to do this. Providing, of course, he was willing to let them. The only chance he could see was to run while he could and every time that he could until he got into those rocks or was dropped. On this conclusion he thrust the cartridges into his pockets, sprang up with his rifle and hit a lope for where Pammy had come to a stop just outside the red buttes marking the entrance to the Valley of Skulls.

He covered some fifty or sixty feet before shouts from those red devils heralded pursuit. He didn't waste energy looking back at them but put everything he had into stretching his stride. It was a killing pace in that kind of heat but he was dead anyway if he didn't get clear, and he kept doggedly going until the spat-spat of lead kicking sand all about him and the burst-bellows wheeze of each torturing breath forced him once more to drop.

He got off six shots before his vision quit spinning, and then threw two more before they pulled out of range, and considering his rep it was damned poor shooting. Only one 'good' Indian and two shot horses to show for eight shells. And the rest of them now had come back for the finish, howling and shooting like a bunch of drunk squaws as they flashed on past in a strungout circle.

Olds hugged the ground through a hail of bullets, never lifting his head till they began to slack off as guns were shot empty. Coming onto a knee then, he dropped one more as they streaked off to reload.

So far, plainly, he had got all the best of it, but his muscles were jumping and he was still some four hundred yards from the rocks where Pammy stood nervously watching. It looked an awful long way with the dust from those Injuns still coloring the air. He jerked the slack from his belt and took off again, running close to the ground as he could get in his hurry; and once again he was stopped by the shrill scream of pellets. This time when he dropped, sweat-soaked and gasping, the rock-ribbed entrance looked not much over two hundred yards off — about seventy strides if you were anxious enough.

He hadn't had much time to think about the girl but — so far as he could see — she hadn't come to yet. She was still belly down, not doing any noticeable wriggling. She was gnawing him more than he was ready to consider — not that *any* dame wouldn't who'd been through what she had!

The Apaches were forming to come at him again, and not wasting much breath getting at it this trip. Pammy, both ears up and with neck stretched like a stalking cat, disappeared with his burden between the red buttes.

Barney jerked his head round as, with bloodcurdling yells, the Indian wheel began to spin once more, faster and wilder as they narrowed in on him, superb in their horsemanship, firing under the necks of their mounts as they flashed past.

Down flat, gritting his teeth in a snarl of frustration, Olds fingered his trigger with eyes thinned to slits as he impatiently waited for something to line sights on. It was while he lay waiting that he grimly remembered he had failed to load his piece after the last charge.

The cast of his cheeks showed an uncontrolled violence as the precariousness of this went through him like fire. Besides the shell in the chamber, his rimfire weapon held not over seven loads.

This could get pretty sticky before it got better — *if* it did!

Angrily then, blackly leading his target, he

knocked over a horse, and another, and two more. Three of those bucks scrambled up, one of them limping but still clutching his rifle. Olds sent that one sprawling. Drove another one spinning into a drunken stagger and emptied his Henry at the third without scoring.

Belatedly, then, through drifts of smoke, he saw the wave of still-mounted Apaches driving straight at him.

Snarling defiance he reached for his belted six-shooter and the scrabble of fingers found empty leather. The pistol was gone! Staring into those yelling, paint-hideous faces, Olds crazily grinned and prepared to die.

X

But not without company!

Reversing the rifle — no great trick for a man left one-handed in a two-fisted world — Barney fastened his grip round the end of the barrel and, despising them, waited for something to get within reach.

The whole scope and style of this operation bugged him.

It wasn't like Injuns to beat a dead horse or like Apaches to suffer so great a decimation just to come at and torture one lousy stinking paleface — not even with an olive-skinned woman to give it frosting. Not even, by God, if he was the most hated White Eyes this side of the Happy Hunting Grounds. Not even conceding vengeance to be at the bottom of so all-out an effort.

Sure, they hated his guts, understanding all too probably the reason for his continuing forays into their heartland. Nothing odd about that. What Olds *couldn't* understand was this sudden great froth to cook his goose right here and now when he was already bound with plainly obvious haste to put himself and his red-lipped woman within the rock jaws of the waterless oven which — certainly within their memory — had claimed the lives of so many hated White Eyes.

But Olds had no time to jaw around with this now. He stepped away from the Henry, barrel at arm's length, determined to hold back his swing until there was no chance of missing.

They weren't firing now. They wanted to ride him down, take him with enough life left in his carcass to make sure he took a good while with his dying.

But someone apparently was too vengeful or eager to heed the chief's dictum. A rifle began racketing through the vicious undulations. Still three yards short of Barney's reach the nearest brave, reeling, pitched sideways off his horse. Pretty lousy shooting, he thought, as another one, screeching, fell off his mount backwards. Then Bloody Head himself loomed towering above Olds, and Barney's swung rifle took him squarely in the chest. The blow knocked most of the yell out of his mouth but failed to unhorse him and he slammed on past as another buck, lunging, carried Barney to the ground in a furious thrashing of arms and legs. Someway, during that grunting tangle, Barney's face was shoved smotheringly into the loose sand but he managed to roll clear. Before he could scramble up the brave's bony knees crashed into his chest, knocking him back. Gasping, he felt the knees straddle his waist and caught, half-blinded, the downward streak of steel coming at him, twisting barely in time to see it flash past his cheek, grounded to the hilt by the drive of that arm.

Before the Indian could snatch it free Barney's grip closed round that copper wrist like a vise, let it start up and then, reaching for breath, hammered it desperately — twisting as he did so — against the man's naked chest. The Apache, gurgling, folded limply across him as blood gouted hotly from the gaping wound.

Olds wriggled clear and, eyes streaming, staggered erect to find the fellow's surviving comrades kicking their horses through a fantail of dust across the crest of a ridge some hundred yards off. It was a most welcome sight, for he was too tired even to shake a fist after them. He was so goddam weak the knees buckled under him and — while he didn't pass out — he never even noticed the continued banging of that rifle until the sound of it quit.

That fetched his head up and he saw the black smoke still hanging like tatters of gunmetal mist against the red rock of the portal's nearest butte. So he reckoned he'd had help, and wondered how the girl had got herself loose . . . and abruptly stared harder as it soaked through his cabeza the girl hadn't any gun. Not a rifle, certainly.

He got onto his feet, scooped up his hat and, as he started for the rock, some portion of his customary alertness crept through the exhaustion of battle and he jerked a dull glance about. A pretty expensive business for sure.

The red raiders' casualties had been extraordinarily heavy. Not over five of those bastards had rode off the field. Bloody Head's face must be dragging the ground after a setback like this. And, unless he came

80

back to pick up his dead, his red brothers were like to stage an open rebellion.

Barney grinned with satisfaction. He'd been powerful lucky, all things considered, and may well have toppled Bloody Head into permanent disrepute with the tribe. In any event, he would be a long while working up sufficient enthusiasm to ramrod them savages into another pass at El Mocho.

But his grin whizzed out as he peered toward the buttes. Something uncommon odd about the help he had got from that hidden rifle. He couldn't recollect leaving any weapons at the cache, only water, grub and cartridges. Anyway, he'd tied her on pretty good. Didn't seem likely she had got herself loose. And, even if she had, she couldn't know about the cache. And sure as hell not where to *find* it!

There had to be someone else on that butte. And a pretty fair shot to give those Apaches a bellyful!

He gave it up in disgust. He'd find out quick as ever he got there. He was glad for the help but could think of a deal of things he'd prefer to more company. Five years of lone-wolfing it, of fending for himself, made the prospect of company considerable less than welcome.

It would mean putting off his hunt for a spell, and he didn't have any use for a partner. He had no desire or intention of sharing any part of Yuma's gold if he came onto it. He didn't want nobody around when he uncovered it. Company could only complicate things — like that dang female woman!

Maybe he could palm her off on the guy. He could see one thing sure as last year's leaves. The stuff he had at this cache — freighted in at great cost of sweat and cash outlay — would go a heap farther one way than three. He supposed he could spare the feller a meal — grudgingly reckoned he owed him that much; but grub wasn't in such abundance he could waste it.

Plodding on with his problems, fussing and fuming, Olds — trying to think how he could quickest be rid of him — finally hardened his heart. There was just one way to handle this bum. Fill up his gut and tell him to shove off.

Feeling some better Barney firmed up his jaw, and was still grimly minded to brook no nonsense when, limping between the two great rocks — still lugging his empty Henry repeater — he strode through the hundred-foot passage and came into the red valley to find the guy waiting beside a roan horse.

He had Pammy and the girl — on her feet — alongside him.

This much Olds saw before the girl's stormy look and the unfocused pistol loosely held in the feller's hand drew his widening glance to that grinning face.

There was nothing friendly about it. The skin twisted across that double row of teeth was more remindful of fox or coyote than of anything Olds would have picked as human.

The pistolman chuckled maliciously. "I don't reckon you expected to meet up with me so soon again. Let go of that rifle — and don't try anything."

Olds wasn't about to try anything, not with that six-shooter eyeing his briskit. More puzzled than worried, he put the Henry carefully down, trying to think what ailed this dang fool and where their tracks could have previously crossed.

"Now — step away from it."

"Hell, it ain't loaded," Barney sneered, complying. And then his eyes bugged a little. There was something about that voice, a certain cadence or timber — some damn thing, which reminded him strangely of the guy who had braced him coming out of the gloom of that Camp Grant gateway; and a cold chill developed somewhere south of his belt.

It was him, all right. That sonofabitch smuggler! The nut who had claimed Olds had jumped his girl!

XI

Barney, remembering, felt the pull of his breath beginning to tighten as some of the more colorful of this border ruffian's didos unfolded across the shortened circuits of his mind.

Then, angrily, he took hold of himself. Anyone could look tough behind the snout of a gun. Slick he might be, and tricky too, but tough was something that had to be proved and this weasel hadn't the frame to stand up to the kind of hard knocks a guy working grubstakes took as a matter of course. As for the yarns . . . well, hell! Olds knew what stock you could put in stories, having been, over the years, the butt of many himself. Mostly they was nothing but a pack of dang lies!

So he shrugged and stepped back, biding his chance, saying in a sullen, defeated tone of voice: "If this is a stickup, chum, you're wastin' yer time. I ain't got the price of a postage stamp on me. Hell — look for yourself!" and turned out his pockets which, except for the forgotten rimfire cartridges, held nothing but junk.

The smuggler's twisted grin, broadening across the bulge of big teeth, derided him. Shrugging, Barney said, "Well, if it's supplies you're after, provisions — that stuff . . ."

Goyanno guffawed. "Very fonny." But the tawny eyes behind that hooked beak pushed no laugh wrinkles into the brown skin of his cheeks. That cold snaky glitter was cruelly yellow as a cat's, and in the grip of that look Olds remembered Camp Grant and the unfinished business the corporal's guard had busted up. It was not a comforting reminder in the focus of that pistol.

Goyanno pointed. "Let's see how *rápido* you can take your feet to those cliffs off there at the back of thees place. *Andar! Pronto!*"

Nervously shifting, Barney stared.

"Oh — go!" the girl cried in an agony of fright. "Can't you see he is aching to *kill* you?"

Olds hadn't got quite that far in his assessment, but the assumption didn't seem at all farfetched. He wasn't the kind, however, to be easily stampeded. "If he'd wanted me dead, why'd he bother —"

"To chase off *los Indios?* Ho!" Goyanno sneered. "I did not do eet for you."

85

Something in the contemptuous slanch of that stare lifted Olds' look from the smuggler to the girl. It was the smell of fear coming from her that suddenly aroused him, told him the truth. It was on account of her Goyanno had chipped in to help him drive those redskins off; and he recalled with a strange surprise the colonel telling him this two-bit contrabandista had claimed the girl for his own. It sure hadn't looked that way to Olds but, regardless of what the facts of this was, it was readily apparent she was terrified now.

Barney wasn't feeling too brash himself, not with that hogleg so unwinkingly eyeing him.

"*Vamanos, gringo!* Hit up a lope before I empty thees gon at you!"

There didn't seem to be much else Barney could do, but he was danged if he'd run.

Hitching up his pants with a scowl he set off. But after five or six strides with the glare of that feller burning into his back, pride didn't look so important as it had. He broke into a run in spite of himself when the first blue whistler sailed past his ear.

After he'd got out of range he slowed enough to peer back. Enraged to see Goyanno cuffing the girl around, Olds slid to a stop, and right then the bastard hit her with his fist hard enough to send her sprawling.

Incensed by such behavior Barney started back. The contrabandista, looking up, saw him before he'd gone ten jumps and grabbed the rifle off his saddle. Still riled, panting curses but not quite ready to welcome wings and a harp, Barney put on the brakes. The first slug kicked sand across his boots and the next went through his hat like a hornet. Olds, not waiting for a third, took off and, this time, the effort really heated up his axles.

When he finally figured he'd got far enough to quit he was too far away to do anything about it when Goyanno, now mounted, forced the girl — with a rope around her neck — to climb astride Pammy and head on out of the canyon.

Too beat to cuss, Olds watched them go with oddly mixed emotions. It would have been hard to say which griped him the most, loss of the burro or the compelled departure of that featherheaded frail — though *he* wasn't in any doubt, of course.

It would have riled him, naturally, to see *any* woman manhandled in such fashion, treated like a chattel.

But in the scale of crimes most frowned on hereabouts there were few things more calculated to invite general wrath and speedy retribution than deliberately to remove a feller's means of transportation. This, in the West, was the epitome of wickedness.

And Olds was properly shocked.

Matter of fact, he was downright furious. Sure he'd got accustomed to hiking it — the accepted *modus operandi* of sheepherders and prospectors — and he could, like as not, have counted on one hand the times he'd found it incumbent to climb on old Pammy; but who was to say when having that critter might not be all that stood between himself and some goddam lonely grave? — a miserable death even?

And there was a personal angle. Come right down to it, this four-footed friend was the only really loved thing Barney'd ever latched onto — all the 'family' he'd known. It was a heinous thing to part a gent from his loved one!

But as he limped on back to where he'd set out from, he got to thinking more and meaner about that son of a buck forcing the girl to go with him. Somehow, uneasily, he got to wondering if most of the meanness he felt wasn't someway related to the way he had treated her. And this, of course, opened the door to a whole flock of notions he wasn't ready to reckon with.

He was in a pretty obstreperous mood time he got to the big rock behind which, a good while ago, he'd buried the things he'd been aiming all day for, the holecards through which he had figured to confound his copper-skinned enemies.

With this hidden water and himself comfortably stashed in the gut of that passage with his trusty rifle he could have turned back the U. S. Cavalry if need be — leastways long as his grub held out.

Shelving those aggravating thoughts of Carmella along with his own unacknowledged culpability he came around the rock and laboriously moved a plethora of smaller ones, grumbling and scowling like a sore-footed bear.

Hunger and thirst grew apace in him now as he resentfully considered the packed and stubborn soil he had stomped in so firmly under this thin spread of sand. He devoutly wished now he'd not so stupidly abandoned the pick and shovel he'd left out there by his pack after tying the girl aboard Pammy. Was even seriously minded to go back after them till he remembered Bloody Head and his surviving Apaches.

It was a sobering thought and scarcely calculated to inspire further waste of time. Dropping onto his knees he brushed away the sand, realizing as he did so he would not get far scrabbling at such unyielding and shaley soil with bare fingers.

It didn't take long, once he'd thought of it, to locate a rib bone in this grisly repository of dead men's relics. He still yearned for his shovel and the pick he'd discarded but the rib was considerably better than fingers. In twenty minutes of gasping, unremitting effort, induced by thirst and the nagging memory of vengeful Apaches, he managed to move enough ground with his desperate scratching to expose one end of the tin which held his water. The grub and cartridges, protected by a stout piece of tarp, were hidden under this and it was too damned bad — as he told himself grumpily — he hadn't thought when planting this stuff to include a gun.

The water container was a five-gallon milk can and he was forced to spend an additional quarter hour sufficiently widening the hole to get a proper grip. Then he got a bad jolt.

Bending down to get hold of the uppermost handle he noticed darkened earth at the sides of the can and the faint dampness of this gave him some pretty bad moments till he got the thing out. It was the lightness of it which confirmed his apprehensions. Yet his look grew fiercely puzzled when he found it stoppered tightly. He stared for a couple of breath-held minutes at the jagged gash along the side before astonished understanding rushed painfully through him. Some son of the devil had taken an axe to it!

XII

He grew so furiously wild when he thought of Goyanno leaving him here without water, gun or burro in this bastardly hellhole of flesh-frying heat he pretty nearly threw a fit. All the blood rushed to his head, and in this red fog of rage he'd have traded every hope of Yuma's gold just to get one fist round the smuggler's throat.

Man, he was mad! He flung the rib bone down so hard it bounced. The packets of flour and beans, salt pork and saleratus so carefully wrapped in the tarp's oiled canvas had been not only ripped open but so wantonly scattered over the bottom of the hole, as to be utterly spoiled. The two boxes of .44 rimfires were gone, disappeared completely.

Then, just as he was about to get up from the hole, a faint slither of sound, dry as curled leaves, pulled his face round to the right. There, just behind him, not two feet from his hip and already coiled, tongue wickedly darting, was the biggest damned diamondback he'd ever clapped eyes on.

Olds was petrified, rigid as a rabbit peering down the gullet of a winter-starved wolf. If he'd had a gun — his shovel even, he might at least have glimpsed a halfway chance of someday telling someone else about it. But what chance did you have against a snake barehanded? — squatted back to it and *one*-handed at that!

He hadn't reckoned he had any perspiration left but could feel sweat cracking through the pores of his skin. He'd been wondering how long the furnace heat in this place would take to cook a man caught here like he was, but eyeing that reptile the only thing he could think of was this god-awful cold that held him frozen in his tracks. One careless move and he could say goodbye to everything.

It was then that he remembered his digging tool, the rib bone he'd flung down in such a passion of fury.

His eyes skittered round trying to pick up the sight of it. Not for all the king's horses would he have moved his head with that coiled death crouched less than two feet from his tingling hip. But he spied the bone

— he had only to move a bare yard to get hold of it.

One yard. Three feet. Scarcely thirty-six inches — one quick lunge and he'd have it. All that held him back was the belly-cramping picture of that goddam snake, for there'd be no turning back, no calling it off if the rattler proved faster.

He certainly couldn't stay here on his hunkers much longer; he was running out of balance.

Desperately Olds scanned his chances and, twisting, dived.

With that rope round her neck Carmella climbed aboard Pammy, too sick and de-spirited to put up much fuss. She had known some rough moments in Tucson's White Horse Bar but at least in that place — though he'd frequently been a bit rough and unpleasant — Goyanno's arrogant advances and unflagging pursuit had, of necessity, been kept within reasonable bounds. Out here in these desolate, sand-drifted wastes . . .

In spite of the heat she could not repress a shiver. She'd had a pretty plain sample of things to come when Peep had knocked her sprawling with a clout from his fist. It was too purely terrifying to speculate about. If she could have seen a fair chance of getting away . . . but no burro was going to outrun a horse. Any hope of help from Olds fled her mind when the smuggler, grabbing up Barney's rifle, beat the barrel out of shape on a rock before mounting.

She sank into herself, pale and hopeless. With the rough feel of the rope painfully chafing her neck she led off as directed, afraid even to let the burro pick his own path lest any divergence from Goyanno's notions drag her off the burro's back.

The smuggler was plainly tickled with himself.

How he had managed to get clear of Camp Grant was hard to figure out unless he'd greased some guard's palm. Or the colonel himself — after she'd been found missing — could have decided to wash his hands of the business; in which case, of course, they'd have turned Peep loose.

Just the same, she acknowledged, it had been pretty shrewd of him to guess Olds' destination and get there ahead of them. His devotion, in less rigorous circumstances, might have been flattering had he been anyone but Goyanno.

But the things she had heard of him, the vivid memory of her own brief exposures, only served to heighten the numbing dread that was threatening to strangle all her initiative. The sheer awfulness of her predicament, trapped out here alone with him, so completely at his scrupleless mercy, was beyond all ordinary spurrings of panic. What was in the cards was going to *be,* regardless.

She was fatalist enough to understand that. One might shudder and quail at the writing on the wall, but her own experience in rebelling against fate had already proved — or so she thought — the uselessness of impulsive resistance. What good had it done her to run away from the White Horse?

This burro, by the looks of him, was pretty well pooped — and small wonder — but Goyanno was in no mood to let him rest. He kept heckling the beast with growls and blows, but every time he let up the burro did too, falling into a shuffling walk until, finally, aggravated beyond endurance, the smuggler spurred on ahead and with never so much as a backward glance, continued to harry his own mount along.

She had been in the deepening despair of self pity, even dully considering doing away with herself if the chance were presented but, faced with the imminence of a broken neck, self-destruction oddly lost its appeal and when the rope began to shut off her wind she frantically booted Pammy into a lope.

Barney knew that if, in his desperate lunge, his legs failed to elude the strike of that snake he might just as well get to work on his death chant. He threw everything he had into carrying himself clear and lit rolling, reaching, coming onto a knee as he grabbed up the rib.

The snake, having missed, was stretched full length, though with plainly no intention of remaining that way. The glittering wickedness of that unwinking stare, the lightning dart of forked red tongue, might have paralyzed a man less inured to danger.

But Barney, looking pretty deadly himself, waited only till the snake made up its mind to get away. As soon as it slithered into motion he was onto it fiercely, savagely beating at its head with the bone.

When he got up he made double certain by grinding its neck under the twist of a heel. After that he was so weak his knees banged together and it was while he was hunting a safe place to flop that a guttural voice came out of the silence, startling him so badly he nearly knocked himself over. What was said he didn't notice; the fact that it was *Indian* was all his mind right then could take hold of.

For what seemed an eternity he stood staring, looking down at the snake's dying wriggles, eyes darting up to peer gingerly about. The Indian sat on a scrawny paint horse with a ghost cord round its jaw and a tailful of cockleburrs. He had a kind of sear singer round the horse's belly that apparently was fastened to the scrap of ragged blanket his naked butt was perched on, and he had the facial bones of a Pima, though the feet at the ends of the dangling legs had been thrust into smoke-darkened Apache boots. Which could mean he was allied by blood or choice, maybe even through marriage.

The Indian said, "You El Mocho. Much hiko. Apaches heat rocks for you," and grinned hungrily.

Olds didn't like the look of him one little bit. And it was more than just that. He was gaunt as a gutted snowbird and about as wild above the beak as a critter that's wintered on loco weed. And he smelled like a wolf den. But mostly it was the rifle that put Olds into such a dither of sweat, the way the old fool was waving it around, finger inside the trigger guard.

If he'd been on the warpath he'd have counted coup already; but a guy could kick off just as quick by mistake and a bullet didn't care who the hell it jounced into!

"What you want?" Barney growled, voice fiercened by concern.

"You give?" the buck said, pointing the gun at him. "No give, mebbe pretty soon kill *you,* too."

Olds finally got it through the whirl of his head it was that whopping big snake the old reprobate wanted. "Hell, take it an' welcome," he piped up, some relieved.

But he couldn't seem to get his eyes off that rifle. It looked new enough, the packing grease scarcely off it, a repeater of the latest and most advanced model. Still thinking about it he went over, picked up the snake by the tail and came back, holding it out to him.

The paint rolled wild eyes, looking ready to bolt.

"Here," Olds said, "you keep." Then, screwing up his nerve: "What name, you? How callum?"

"Charlie!" the old buck grinned, effectively subduing his fractious mount with the ghost cord. "Many coups, me — kill much white mans! You ketch whiskey?"

"No ketchum," Olds reluctantly admitted, still considering the rifle and taxing his brain to find some way of getting the jump here. Must be something the danged renegade would go for. He asked, suddenly inspired: "You like young squaw?" and carved a curvy line through the air with his hand.

There was a great clap of sound and Olds snatched back his fist as flame spat from the rifle, the slug from that blast viciously jerking his hat off.

Like a pair of strange dogs the two glared at each other.

Olds picked up his hat. "What's the matter with that gun?" he demanded when he'd got back enough wind to talk with.

"Alla time go off — *bam! bam!*" the Indian nodded.

"Yeah. Mebbeso take your leg off," Olds pointed out, craftily adding, "Gun like that no good for Injun, all the time make trouble. Here — tell you what I'll do. You throw in with me an' I'll git you another gun, one you kin depend on — how's that sound to you?" and reached out his hand.

But Charlie had heard the owl hoot. He backed his horse away from Olds, bringing up the rifle, fierce eyes glittering. "We swap when you ketchum gun." He grinned. "Where you got squaw?"

XIII

Barney, busy with sour thoughts, did not answer at once. He was still plenty riled, remembering how Goyanno had suckered him, but he wasn't so sure now it had been the smuggler who'd got into his cache and destroyed all the trumps Olds had had up his sleeve. The ground hadn't been wet enough for all that water to have leaked out today. So it must have been Bloody Head's bunch who'd come onto it, maybe watching him bury it, planning to trap him here. And he could still leave his hair in this goddam oven unless he could come to terms with this Pima. Even then too, maybe, but at least he'd have a chance.

Everyone had heard of old Cheek Creek Charlie, the renegade Pima who'd married Bloody Head's sister and had later fallen out with him over division of some spoils. He'd blown a hole through his wife to emphasize his defiance and gone off one dark night with ten of the chief's finest horses. The result was a blood feud which had raged for three years and, while this nizzy old coot by any normal gent's standards might appear about ready for a string of spools, there was nothing much the matter with his defense mechanisms and he had been around long enough to know up from down. And just about there he broke into Barney's cogitations to demand again testily: "Where you got squaw?"

Olds, fetching his mind back, jerked his handless arm toward the canyon's entrance. "One sleep maybe if we set out straightaway," and hoped the wild-eyed old warrior didn't start hunting sign. "While I was gone from this place," he growled, "bad white man stealum, put rope round neck — C'mon, I'll show you," and set off for the buttes.

He wasn't sure Charlie would follow. He wasn't sure about anything except that unless he took after them pretty dang quick Goyanno was like to get clean away with it — could almost hear the son of a bitch bragging. *Sure I took her away from him,* he'd say. *Bloody Head's bunch had the place surrounded, but I got her away from them — fooled the whole push!*

Made him grind his teeth just to think of that bastard.

"How you break rifle?"

Like a dash of cold water Charlie's shout spun him round.

"Oh, that!" he grumbled. "Broke it in the rocks tryin' t' git at that snake. C'mon, if yer comin'." He strode into the gut.

Pretty soon he heard the clatter of the paint horse's hoofs and when they came to the buttes Charlie said behind him, "You wait — me look!"

He slid off the pinto's rump and tossed its tether string to Olds, but took the rifle with him in his sure-footed climb through the rocks. He went up the nearest butte like a monkey and, flat against it, bellied down near the top for a long careful look. "Apaches gone," he called down — "a little dust," and pointed. "More dust, there." He swung an arm toward the south.

That would be the one, Barney reckoned. Goyanno would be making either for Tucson or the border, and most probably the latter. As the image of Carmella came to harrow his troubled thoughts, he fiercely glared at the red emptiness about him. Was it *his* fault she'd gone and got herself run off with? He'd never asked nor wanted to be responsible for her — or for any other dadblamed female. "Women!" he spat, and tied on a few cusswords.

All they ever brought a man was trouble!

"How far?" he called up, so dry in the throat he could scarcely get the sound past, and so fuzzy headed he could just about hear it. But Charlie looked around. Olds' eyes hurt so bad he had to pretty near scrinch them shut, but he caught the flash of the Pima's teeth and the skittery glint of that stolen rifle. It just about had to be stolen; nobody would be a big enough fool to give a dang redskin a weapon like that.

"Two horas mebbe." Charlie started down.

Olds reckoned this heat — no water and all — must finally be getting him; and he was finding it harder to keep his thoughts gathered or make any sense out of them he scraped up. Two hours was stupid with the kind of lead that bastard had got, and them riding double on that scarecrow paint.

The Indian, slithering over the last rock, reached for the tether string, then let the hand drop to push out his wrinkled lips and peer inscrutably into Olds' face. "Better you stay here."

Olds glared back, inflamed eyes trying fiercely to focus, aghast and filled with apprehensions at the idea of this savage riding after them alone. It must be admitted to Barney's credit he hadn't thought of himself left to feverishly expire in the heat-scorched air of this red rock trap. This was one picture that never entered his mind.

It was the thought of Goyanno being caught up with by somebody else that dug spurs in him sharpest, cheated of his revenge by a nizzy old coot with a weapon he couldn't even begin to savvy. That was what hurt; and back of all this was what would happen to Carmella, and he didn't much care for the look of that, either. He might not be responsible for getting her out here, but what he had said about her to Charlie could dang well take a mighty lot of forgetting — especial if this Injun took him serious about it.

It was plain he would fight to prevent being left, and if it wasn't quite pity that peered out of the Pima's stare, it was certainly a look that showed a deal of understanding.

With a shrug he indicated that Barney should mount up. Olds, even in the present stumbling state of his awareness, wasn't too much pleasured with the notion of this Injun climbing up behind, but having no adequate grounds for objection he hauled himself aboard, attempting to hide his doubts and his weakness behind a splutter of mumbled curses.

The Indian, with never a backward look, struck off at a ground-eating stride that pulled the pinto into a trot. Olds felt like his crotch would be shoved through the back of his neck from these bone-shaking jolts but nothing he tried changed the bronc's pace a fraction and he presently gave up, bludgeoned into settling for just hanging on.

One thing he did notice: the direction they were going wasn't south by considerable, but he was too used up to argue about it. It took all of his energy and faltering attention merely to make sure he didn't get pitched off. It did kind of burn him though to observe the apparently effortless ease with which that fool Injun held onto his lead — and him old enough to have been Barney's father.

After an endless eternity of bouncing along on that bone-rack's back it took Olds several seconds after they had stopped to catch up with the fact he wasn't still being pounded. Blinking and groaning he discovered that Charlie, quite close, stood peering up into his face with the intently odd look generally reserved by the paleface fraternity for persons they reckoned didn't have all their marbles.

"Eh?" Barney growled, peering like a gaffed fish. "You say somethin' t' me?"

Cheek Creek Charlie managed a dubious nod. "Charlie say 'White brother wait.' You savvy 'wait'? Me look," he grunted, and started off forthwith toward the crest of a dune some forty yards away.

Barney came sliding down off the horse. His legs folded under him and he collapsed like a drunk in a ludicrous sprawl. But he was up straightaway and, with a snarl of disgust for his gone-to-sleep underpinning, caught the paint's tether string and, half running, half staggering, went scrambling after the departing Pima. The Indian looked round, kind of scowled but stood waiting.

"What's the big idea?" Barney gasped, coming up with him.

Charlie put a grimy finger against his mouth and, leaning closer, angrily hissed: "Shhh! White man heap fool!" and with a scathing contempt turned his back on Olds to go catfooting up the near side of the hillock.

But the things Barney saw in his head were too much for him, or perhaps it was the Pima's gruff dismissal. Mumbling and muttering he went shagging after him, careening along like a ship in full sail on a choppy sea. Once the Indian looked back, fiercely fingering his rifle, then, snarling, went on.

Olds' extravagant exertion, instead of reducing his mobility, appeared to have tapped new reserves of strength. His shambling run grew less erratic. Though he was breathing hard when he went into a crouch he seemed more like his usual crusty self as he dropped down beside the stopped and staring redskin.

The unfolding view proved the Indian's craft but the need for stealth was scarcely apparent. The quarry, plainly in sight less than sixty yards below, was too passionately embroiled to have eyes for anything else. The burro, reared back on his haunches in balky defiance, had evidently refused to be dragged another step.

The rope was off the girl's neck, the smuggler was off his horse, furiously gripping clubbed rifle and wrathily shouting at Pammy's laid-back ears.

Cheek Creek Charlie, peering down the sights, was cuddling his repeater when Olds jerked the weapon away from him. The Pima wheeled with drawn-back lips, reaching for the gun and for his knife simultaneously. "Me killum!" he snarled, eyes mean as the orbs of that broken-backed snake.

"Not this trip, pardner," Barney growled, stepping back to let the old coot have a good hard look down the gut of that barrel. "A dead Injun won't count no more coups on *nobody!* Set easy now an' let a man handle this that savvies hair triggers."

He stepped off three more paces, watchful and wary. The old man was still furious but a lot of the wildness had whizzled out of his stare. Olds pushed home the clincher. "I promised you a gun you could shoot, an' you'll git it." With some of Charlie's own arrogance — risky here — Olds ignored the old man to send a hoarse shout racketing out over the desert. "You, down there — Goyanno! Drop that rifle an' throw up your hands!"

XIV

Down below Peep Goyanno jumped back like a scorpion had crawled up his pantsleg. Then went rigidly still, still gripping his weapon and no doubt wondering if he could get it reversed and whip the sights into focus before Olds could drive a blue whistler through his carcass. To help him decide Barney squeezed off a shot that sent sand rattling across the smuggler's boots.

"Gun's a mite new to me," Barney called, jeering, "but the next one, I betcha, takes off half of that jaw!"

Goyanno let go of the rifle.

"Kick it over to the girl an' then stay put."

The smuggler, grudgingly, obeyed with care; it was plain he wasn't about to get himself skewered on the short end of Barney's temper. Not if he could help it. Nor did he waste any breath in swearing. He stood there meek as Mary's lamb with both hands lifted, swarthy face expressionless.

Olds wasn't deceived into getting careless. He wasn't trusting anyone any farther than he could sling them, least of all this unstable Indian who still had his knife and a habit of impulse not quite as reliable as a case of thawed dynamite.

Barney tossed him the tether string, motioning him on with a flap of the arm. He didn't want nobody behind him right now.

When Goyanno spotted the Indian he appeared to seem a little disquieted, shifting his weight, scuffing round in his boots almost as though he'd half a mind to make a run for it.

Olds put a slug between those braced legs. "Stand hitched," he grumbled. "I ain't tellin' you again — an' step outa that shell belt."

"Oh, Barney!" Carmella gulped, clutching the picked-up rifle as if it were a gatepost she'd come thankfully to lean on. "I — I never expected to *see* you again!" and, with her face wrinkling up, she broke into tears.

Olds scowled, embarrassed but — oddly enough — perked up by it too, though feeling moved to conceal this behind a gruff snort. He snapped at the smuggler with fiercening stare: "Git outa that gun belt or a colander is goin' t' look sploshy beside you!"

Goyanno quit stalling and let the belt drop, a little gray about the gills, eyes beginning to roll like a stallion bronc's when Cheek Creek Charlie suddenly swerved in his direction. *Madre de Dios!* he exclaimed with a gasp. "You goin' t' let this redskin snatch my hair?"

Charlie drew himself up in a huff to say grandly: "Apaches not scalp." Then, contemptuously: "Who want hair of dog-face Mexicano?" and copiously spat. He slanched a glance at Olds. "You killum now?"

Barney chewed at his lip. Then he shrugged and said, "That'll depend on him, how he acts from here out," and saw disbelief in the Pima's face.

Carmella, meanwhile, had got hold of herself. Them tears hadn't done her face much good and the brush they'd been through had about ruined her clothes, but she had good stuff in her, more strength than you'd think to look at her. More damn guts than you could hang on a fencepost.

Aware of Charlie's sullen looks, Olds said to the girl, "Let's have that smokepole." And, anchoring the butt under his handless arm, worked the gritty mechanism, dumping the shells out, dropping all but one cartridge into his pocket. He peered at this a moment and, finally shrugging, put it into the breech and let the hammer down. With a dubious frown he tossed the weapon to the Indian. "You watch out fer that now."

Charlie, all grin, patted the rifle affectionately. "Me careful!"

Olds, grunting, reached for the water bag, and, uncapping it, upended it, letting only a couple of swallows trickle down his parched throat. Then he washed out his mouth and put the bag back.

He went over and caught up the reins of Peep's horse, a rugged looking roan despite its rough and lathered appearance. "Here —" Goyanno said nervously. "What about me?"

"If you're comin' with us you walk," Olds told him; and then, to the rest of them: "Let's git outa here."

The Pima caught hold of his bad arm and pointed.

Olds stared. There was a smoke coming off the top of Old Baldy and, off here north of them, another smoke answering it. He chewed a while at his lip and looked again at Goyanno, seeing the Mexican shiver. "Can't help it," he grumbled. "We're goin' t' have to go back. We better git at it."

He swung onto Peep's roan, the girl got back on the burro and old Charlie, belying his look of great age, vaulted up on his pinto as though scarcely out of his seventeenth summer. Goyanno glowered, but struck off smart enough when his confiscated rifle in the Pima's eager hands swung jerkily to a focus just above his belt buckle.

It was almost dark when they got back to the place where Olds had abandoned his pack, pick and shovel. He found them laying where he'd dropped them. After a hard look at Goyanno, who seemed in pretty bad shape, he stepped down and told the others he was going to camp in this place for a couple of hours to give the mounts some rest and wait for a night breeze before traveling farther.

Actually he was beginning to feel a little sorry for the smuggler, but mostly it was to rest up the girl and make sure the transportation wasn't about to play out on them. Likewise he wanted it to be good and dark before they set out again. He didn't aim for the bastards that was manning them smokes to have any inkling of where he was bound for. He intended to be plumb out of sight before morning. By the time those Apaches got onto his trail again he figured to have enough lead to lose them completely.

He helped himself to some water, then passed the bag around, warning the girl against taking too much of it. Then he got out the grub that was stored in his pack and they all chewed jerky for the next several minutes while Barney turned over a rather fanciful notion he'd latched onto last night and which had only just now come back to him. When they got done with their eating he took the Pima aside.

He was a little reluctant to jog the old duffer's memory but guessed, long as he kept his wits about him, he had ought to be a match for anyone old as Charlie with a jammed-up rifle that held only one cartridge — and which, if fired, would likely prove more deadly to the one who pulled the trigger than to anybody else.

"Charlie," he said, man to man fashion, "you recollect that pony soldier feller married into the Arivaipas back a spell when old Pascual was chief? Feller they called Yuma?"

Charlie tugged on his nose. "Savvy Yuma, sure."

"Whereabouts was the tribe when he married Pascual's daughter?"

The Pima rubbed at his dirt-filled

wrinkles, peered at Olds more closely, settled his Injun look more securely in place and abruptly belched. The smell was even worse, if anything, but Olds bore it manfully and waited, thinking to have caught a crafty gleam behind that stare.

"Red Rock?" Charlie offered it solemnly, but Olds only snorted. "Don't play games with me, old man. I wasn't born yesterday."

The Pima, scratching himself, eyeing Barney inscrutably, showed his teeth in a wolfish grin. "You huntum yellow iron?"

"Well — yeah."

Charlie nodded. "Long time you huntum. No find. Bad luck, that stuff. Many peoples dead."

Olds, pondering, finally shrugged. Turning away he said over his shoulder, "Don't guess you know as much as I figgered. Just another dumb Injun without enough sense to git outa the rain. Don't know why the hell I wanted you fer a pardner," he growled disgustedly, starting back toward Carmella and the glowering smuggler.

He heard the redskin grunt. A copper arm snaked out and hauled him around. The Indian's eyes were like hot coals. "Me — you — all same brother?"

"Forget it," Olds said. "I'll find me another boy. Some schoolboy with savvy —"

"Me savvy!" hissed Cheek Creek Charlie. "You shake? Ketchum gold, ketchum whiskey?"

Barney peered at him again, shook his head. "Too dumb, you —"

"Me *show!*" Charlie snarled, grabbing hold of him again.

Appearing to hesitate, still looking dubious, Olds said doubtfully, "Hell, you're a Pima, you're no Apache. You got no more idea where that gold is than I have."

But Charlie stubbornly held onto him, drew him down into a squat and with the point of his knife drew some lines in the sand. Breathing hard, he punched a hole along one. "Soldier camp." Then he moved the blade over to a grouping of other marks that looked like little mountains but were probably intended for something else entirely. "One sleep," the Pima grunted and dug his knife in again. "Apache village." His hot eyes came up and both of them grinned.

Charlie rubbed a hand across the picture and the two stood up. "Ketchum squaw?" he growled.

Barney's grin turned stiff. He'd forgot about that. But he said smoothly enough, "Later, mebbe. We'll have to see how this works out." He didn't like the way that Injun was eyeing him, like he was remembering something nasty. "I'll be thinkin' about it."

"Ketchum whiskey?"

"Hell, if we come onto that gold I'll git you a wagonload."

They considered each other and finally clasped hands.

XV

Carmella, in these loneliest minutes of this interminable day, with the mile-long mauves of peak-bent shadows huddled like sleeping sheep on the desert, found grim opportunity to examine in some depth the condition of her world since quitting the White Horse.

Aching in every joint, it occurred to her to wonder if she had not swapped the witch for the devil. Olds held the key and — might as well face up to it — Olds didn't want her — had made that plain. She was not even sure she still wanted *him,* though the promise he held was still manifest, more important now than it had seemed back in Tucson. Yuma's chimney — that golden dream — was all she could find to cling to now, and if it was ever to be found, Olds, she was sure, would be the one to uncover it.

Huddled in her rags, confused by frightening visions, she considered the man in the light of the legend, and was forced to acknowledge he was still an enigma. He was proud, a braggert, he was full of windy oaths; and yet, despite his failures, there was this doggedness about him, this tough strand of stubborn persistence. Five years of unremitting effort had gone into his search; the implications of this could not lightly be discounted. The man was hounded by debts he'd run up and ignored, by jeers and bitter threats, indomitable as time. She could not believe him an utter fool — no one could be that crazy, she thought.

With the fading light a cooling wind came down off the ridgetops to tousle her hair and rattle the grass clumps; and she peered at him, covertly striving to peel the nonsense of fictions from the bedrock of fact.

He didn't care about women. Demonstrably untrue — at least it graveled him to see any woman mistreated; there was a deep thread of chivalry running through the woof of him. He refused to let the needs of women clutter up his own pursuits and this, she told herself, was the size of it, and could not help but feel the challenge.

As night approached Olds ordered the Indian to scrounge up some wood, grass — anything that would burn and throw off some light. And as the evening slowly wasted away he put the animals on picket ropes and gave every sign of preparing to make a night of it. A dry camp, and an exposed one; he presently built up a cautious fire, brightening it enough to show at some distance but small enough to hide what they were actually about.

Full dark fell within short minutes of the sun's disappearance. The wind kicked up and grew gustily belligerent and still Olds sat, determined to rest the animals for as long as he could. He was not surprised at the Pima's revelation, was only astonished he'd not considered this before. Only recently he'd realized Apaches were too nomadic to stay overlong in any one place. This was something, apparently, no one else had remembered — as it applied, at least, to the location of Yuma's chimney.

One sleep from Camp Grant.

Sure, he'd known this all the time. Everyone had known it, and probably known, as he had, that the general direction had been north of east. It was the location of Pascual's headquarters which had thrown off most of the searchers gophering this range. He was sure he could pinpoint that chimney now to within a boundary of two or three miles. It had to be rough country, cut up with more than ridges, for it was somewhere close to the mountains overlooking the San Pedro valley. Like everyone else he'd got his mountains mixed up and tried to come at the treasure from the wrong direction.

He knew better now. Old Charlie's map had straightened him out.

Even so, there was no chance at all of going right at it. First they had to lose those Apaches — the scouts on the rimrocks who'd been sending up signals, and the war party sure to be nosing his tracks. He'd got to get him some grub, a stock to go on with. And they'd have to have water — it was dire need for this that kept sticking the pins in him. Without grub they might manage, but the canteens were empty. Nothing could move or long endure in this country without water — the very air sucked it out of you.

Which meant he'd got to strike for and open up another cache.

The sun went down like a sinking ship out there beyond the rim of the world. Brief twilight faded into full dark and lost itself beyond the glint of the fire. It was time to go, and one by one, the Indian first and Olds moving last to keep an eye peeled for treachery, they slipped away from this camp and got themselves mounted, Olds taking Goyanno up in front of him reluctantly, hat-ing the strain this put on the man's horse. But the roan was big, in better shape than Charlie's paint. And this pipsqueak smuggler looked about done in.

Olds didn't like the feel of this wind. Glad of the welcome coolness it brought he was edgily gnawed by the lifting force of it, the sudden shifts in direction, the cutting sting of it and what it might do if it reached gale proportions. A couple hours of this could play hell with these horses; if it started lifting sand they could be in bad trouble.

He left Charlie in the lead, not bothering the Pima with unnecessary instructions. The old gaffer knew all he needed to for now and was no more anxious to be come onto by Apaches than Barney was himself. Not with visions of promised whiskey to whet his ingenuity.

An hour dragged past without change, without incident. Bloody Head's tribesmen would be watching that fire for as long as they could see it, at least the scouts on the peaks would. The chief, with any reinforcements he'd been able to muster, would be moving in on it, getting himself set to attack at first light, and might or might not discover their flight short of morning. In any event, not even that old fox's sharp eyes could pick out tracks in the black of night.

If this snarling wind didn't undo his plans Olds and his party should be a far piece from there by the time he'd be able to take up their trail. With luck they could be plumb out of sight.

But Pammy and these horses were in no shape to be pushed, short of sheer desperation. He'd have felt a lot better if the wind had turned cold, but it wasn't. The temperature had dropped, but not enough to be of any real help. And overhead the stars were beginnnng to disappear, indicating clouds. Olds sure didn't want no storm to foul him up. They had a lot of ground to cover.

They rode in silence, each busy with his own thoughts, Goyanno doubtless racking his head to find some way of turning the tables. Olds' respect for the girl steadily increased. Never a whimper, not a peep out of her. He didn't see how she stood it; it was all he could do not to groan himself. But he wished, by God, just the same, she wasn't with them.

Hour after hour they moved on through the night, stumbling with weariness when Olds at last called a halt. If he had calculated right they should be about as near as they'd get to the takeoff point where they'd have to swing west to reach the closest buried water. He ordered everybody down for a half hour's rest.

He went over and dropped into the sand alongside the girl, too dry for talk, almost too pooped to think. But his mind kept turning over regardless, pushing new problems at him like he didn't have worries enough as it was. What if there wasn't any water at this next cache? What if them redskins was there waiting for him?

Find out soon enough, he reckoned, when they got there.

The girl pushed herself up. "Do you find me repugnant?"

For a while he just lay there, finally twisting around. "I ain't so good on this habla stuff — try me in English."

"You know what I mean. Why don't you like me?"

He couldn't make out much of her face in this dark. "I like you all right," he said gruffly, stretching out again, trying to find softer ground for his aches.

"You don't act or sound overjoyed at my being here."

Grunting, Olds growled, "You got that much straight."

"But aside from my being a woman —"

"Ain't that reason enough?" Olds growled. "What you done at that post ain't improved any prospects I had for credit — you really fixed my clock with that colonel! Prob'ly got patrols out beatin' the bushes — every post an' sheriff notified in a hundred miles!"

"But as long as I'm with you that won't make any difference; I could tell them the truth."

"Maybe," he said skeptically, "if they'd take time to listen. I could dang well be shot before they got around to hearin'."

"But I can *help* you," she cried, and put a hard lump of something into his hand. So close she leaned he could feel the flutter of her breath on his cheek. In his sudden confusion her lips brushed his ear. "Do you know what that is?" She spoke so low he figured maybe he was imagining it.

For eight or ten heartbeats he stared narrow-eyed. "You say —" he could hardly get the words past the dryness of his throat, "it's a piece of the ore Yuma took from that chimney?"

He saw the bob of her head. "*What* chimney?" he growled.

"That Arivaipa chimney of Apache gold."

XVI

Olds' jaw dropped and he stared, dumbfounded, a rash of crazy questions stampeding through his paralyzed mind. The implications of her statement were too astounding, too far reaching to be encompassed in a moment.

Apparently realizing this she sank back on her haunches, giving him time to get hold of himself, presently murmuring, "I want you to keep it and think about it, Barney. When it's light enough, look at it, study it — perhaps you know where there's a piece you could compare it with. You're going to find I'm right."

He was still flabbergasted, more so if anything. The questions kept banging around in his head, and his heart thumped so loud he couldn't hardly hide the shaking.

He was powerfully tempted to strike a match, but that was one piece of craziness he refused to give in to. "Where'd you git it?" he growled, tone freighted with suspicion.

He saw the shine of her teeth when she shook her head at him. "I don't think," she said quietly, "we've come to that just yet. When you're ready to admit it came from the chimney we'll talk about a partnership —"

"So!" observed Olds, and snorted. "You must think I'm soft in the head!"

"I may come to think so if you keep on being so stubbornly ridiculous. Just point out one time when my being along has in any way hampered you. Well?"

"How about them horse soldiers?" Olds demanded. "You think they'd be camped on my trail except for you?"

She got up and peered around. "I don't see any soldiers. I haven't seen any since we left Camp Grant."

"No credit to you!" Barney fumed. "An' what about this Goyanno pelican? If you didn't fetch him down on me —"

"I suppose I did, but not intentionally. When I got out of Tucson I naturally thought —"

"Some lovers," Olds gruffed, "is hard to git shut of."

He heard the gasp that came out of her. "He has never been that! I don't have any lovers —"

"Then how come he follered you clean t' Camp Grant?"

While she stood glaring down at him it suddenly came over him he had the answer right in his hand — that dang chunk of ore she claimed had come from Yuma's chimney! It was the only thing that made sense to him because the smuggler never would have knocked her round like he had if he'd had any interest in the girl as such. He said, belligerent: "You show this t' him?"

125

"No — I mean not intentionally."

"But he's had a look at it — knows you've got it!"

"I never told him where it came from," she protested.

She wouldn't of had to, Olds thought pityingly. Goyanno had been plying his trade long enough to know jewelry rock when he saw it. He was not a plumb fool.

Samples of Yuma's find were still around, like that chunk on display in the Jacobs Brothers' Pima County Bank down around Meyer and Pennington in Tucson which the smuggler must have seen at least a hundred times. Lucky George Sullivan had one, there was another in the sheriff's office, and the White Horse Bar had a piece of the stuff.

It was distinctive, enough so that no one with half an ounce of savvy would be likely to mistake it for anything but ore from Yuma's chimney. It wasn't any wonder he'd been paying her attention or come after her so quick. So — get rid of the girl and he'd be rid of Goyanno.

Perhaps she was onto the trend of his thinking. Whatever the reason she said, spider soft: "I'm not fooling you, Barney. We'd make a pair to draw to. I could be a real help. More than you know about."

He could tell by the feel and heft it was

ore. He came onto one knee, peering hard at her now, blowing through his nostrils like a disquieted pack pony. "Just name me one way."

"You'd have someone at your back you could trust."

"Yeah," he said, snorting. "Like a snake in my bosom!"

"All right," she replied, suddenly cool. "You're going to need a grubstake. Where do you think to find one now that Mr. Sullivan has publicly disavowed you?"

While he was wrestling with that she said, even quieter, "I can let you have enough to keep you going."

Of all the outrageous statements he had heard from this frail, Olds figured that was one to cap them all; and yet, somehow, against his every intention and all his gnawing suspicions, he found himself believing. The steadiness of her look, the very coolness of her tone, carried conviction.

While he stood there, goggling, Peep Goyanno came drifting over and Olds, slanching a harassed scowl at him, gruffly gave the order to mount up. "Take the lead, Charlie. We'll head west, barking a line on Picacho Peak until I tell you different. You next, Goyanno. Git movin'."

The man bared his teeth when Olds said,

"You'll walk," and waved Carmella up onto his roan. The Mexican looked a heap inclined to argue but abruptly set off without saying a word. Olds, getting hold of the burro's halter rope, walking himself, brought up the rear.

The wind suddenly quit. Trapped heat came off the sandy ground as though someone had opened the door of a furnace. And it was like to get worse before it got any better, Olds reflected as they wound, single file, down into a long and platter-like depression from which higher earth lifted the black shapes of mesas against the leaden, cloud-filled sky.

He found it hot work afoot. But this was a good place to lie doggo during the daylight hours. There were no springs or seeps in this sink to attract Indians and not more than three miles lay between them right now and the cache he'd been making for. If no one had got into it he had five big cans of water buried there, plus several tins of corned beef. Just thinking of that water did a lot toward reviving him. That tinned beef though . . . how far and how long would it last split four ways? Not much longer than a June frost at Tucson!

It was at this point that Olds began seriously and with considerable reluctance to consider the girl as a possible partner. It went sourly against the grain of his beliefs — against all the notions his experience had bred — but one thing was certain. He had either to someway wangle more grub or mighty soon cut the size of his party.

He was loath to part with that Pima just yet. Goyanno was the logical one to get rid of. He spelled nothing but trouble but Barney couldn't quite unscrew himself to the point of turning the son of a bitch loose on the desert. Not that it wouldn't be justice all right. It was what the smuggler had done with him, and Olds was sure enough sorely tempted. He just didn't reckon the girl would hold still for it.

He did briefly wonder what difference her views made. *He* was running this show — don't let no one think different. He guessed he just wasn't up to fussing with her over it, putting up with her nagging. If he found it important to look good in her eyes he was a considerable way from being ready to admit it.

He got them presently camped in the mouth of a draw thickly screened by an overhang of ancient half-dead cottonwoods three feet around and gnarled as Methuselah. He'd spent a deal of time here in the past five years and never once run into anyone. Nobody, without they came plumb onto the rimrocks, would be likely to spot them holed up here.

Day was a grayness above the sink's eastern rim time they'd got the animals hobbled, and the girl and Goyanno had thrown themselves down in a stupor of exhaustion when Charlie slipped off to have a look around. Olds, ejecting and pocketing the shells from the confiscated repeater and with the smuggler's belted six-shooter strapped about his hips, picked up the pick and shovel and headed for his cache.

XVII

He was so weak with relief — or from the heaviness of this labor on an empty gut — that when his shovel dully clanked against an obviously full can he staggered back onto his butt, too taken over by shakes to do anything else. At least they weren't going to die of thirst . . . not straight off, anyway.

If he and Carmella reached an agreement he could send Cheek Creek Charlie off to pack in supplies from Winkelman or Mammoth, he was thinking, when a stone clinked back of him. It was the barest whisper of sound but he whirled up off his haunches like an unwinding rattler, reaching hipward as he did so — too late to grasp the hand that tore the pistol from his holster.

A dizzy multitude of things — none of them useful — flashed through Olds' mind like squares on a crazy quilt as he completed the turn, coming stiffly erect to bitterly stare at the man he'd dehorned, Peep Goyanno with a grin on his face like a hungry wolf.

"Go on," Barney grimaced. "Shoot an' git it over."

"Oho — do not rosh me," the smuggler said, nastily chuckling. "An' do not be anxious, my one-fisted frien'. I will keel you for sure weeth a great deal of pleasure. But first we weel talk . . . there are — how you say? — questions? One can die weeth dignity or die ver-ry hard."

Behind the gun Goyanno laughed. "You comprehend?"

Olds comprehended he was in a real bind and bobbed his head in a reluctant nod. Only chance he could see was to play for time in the hope old Charlie might someway come up and divert this bastard's attention. It wasn't too likely but, "All right," he grumbled, "let's have 'em."

Goyanno's grin broadened. "The girl weel not help you; she ees tap on the head an' ees fas' asleep. An' the Indio, she ees up on the mesa. I 'ave sharp ears, my frien'. Eef you wan' to die easy you weel talk like I say."

"Git on with it," Olds growled.

"For long time you 'ave hunt for the gold of that Yuma — no?"

Barney nodded.

"But thees Indio, she 'ave make map for you — marks een the sand. Make the marks now for Peep."

Olds said, disgusted, "He's got no more idea where that gold is than you have. He was showin' me where Pascual's main camp used to be —"

"Show Peep."

Barney glowered, extending this stubbornness as long as he dared. When the knuckles of Goyanno's trigger hand whitened he dropped back on his bootheels and with one calloused finger began to draw painstakingly.

"An' the holes?"

"Camp Grant," Barney grumbled, putting a finger to the first of them. "Pascual's village," he said, indicating the other. "One sleep."

"An' the chimenea?"

"Chimney? The gold you mean? He dunno where it's at — hell, ask him yourself."

The smuggler stared like he thought Olds was lying, anger coming darkly into his cheeks. He appeared to be having a struggle with himself. Grip tightening on the gun he said: "The ore the girl gave you!" and shoved out his other paw.

Olds made out to be struggling with *him-self* but finally, swearing, rummaging round in a pocket, dragged out the lump and tossed it in such a way it dropped just short of that outstretched hand.

Olds, appraising that furious glance, was preparing to fling himself desperately aside when a stone — coming silently out of the air — struck Goyanno in the head, knocking him into a reeling stagger.

Barney tore into him like a she-catwampus. Before the smuggler knew what was happening he was flat on his back, Olds standing over him with the gun in his fist.

"You kin bet that ain't goin' t' happen again!"

He looked riled enough to kick in the man's ribs — indeed he half raised a boot, towering over the smuggler, glaring, holding it drawn back perhaps twenty seconds before, with a growl, he reluctantly lowered it.

"Since you're feelin' so lively, you can git out them cans an' anythin' else you see in there. Hop at it now — pronto! An' don't give me no backchat or I'm like to forgit there's a lady present!"

It was the only acknowledgement made of Carmella's presence or timely intervention. Still glowering, he booted the shovel at Goyanno as the smuggler was gingerly picking himself up.

The fellow looked about as mean as a trod-on centipede with chillblains. His face was somewhat paler and there was blood on his head but the look on Olds' cheeks indicated there'd be more if he got any loose talk contrary to orders.

Picking up the shovel Goyanno stepped past him and began widening the hole. Olds, still gripped by temper or the fright he'd been given, growled at the girl: "You've got yourself a deal. How long've we got to wait t' git started?"

Looking a little surprised, but gratified too, she stared a moment; then, shrugging, said, "You mean when can I have the money available?"

"When kin I draw on it?"

"How much do you want?"

"Couple hundred will do fer a starter."

The Pima stepped catlike out of the brush with Goyanno's rifle, making a hand sign at Olds; and Carmella said, "It's available now if you're ready to draw up the partnership papers."

Olds said, scowling: "Ain't my word good enough?"

"Your word's all right with me," she nodded, "but a partnership has to deal with other people and some might ask to see my credentials before deciding how much credit —"

Olds broke in testily. "Then you ain't got the cash —"

"Certainly I've got it. It's on deposit at Jacobs Brothers in Tucson. Did you really suppose I'd be ramming around with two hundred dollars tucked in my stocking top?"

Olds flushed, embarrassed. It was plain this frail didn't care what she said. It seemed equally plain she had him over a barrel, and the knowledge did nothing to sweeten his temper. "Well — no," he conceded, and his eyes stabbed around hunting something to kick. It was the same every time he had truck with female; he always wound up with the short end of the stick.

He shot her a measuring glance. "Well, it's been nice knowin' you," he growled at her sourly, "but I ain't got no paper so I guess the deal's off." He blew the drip from his nose and dragged a sleeve across scraggly cheeks. "The roan an' ol' Charlie should see you safe back t' Tucson —"

"I'm staying right here. At least," she said

coolly, eyes flashing defiance, "I'm staying with *you.* I've got paper you can write on."

"You got a pencil, too?"

She ignored his sarcasm. "Goyanno has," she said.

Olds glared blackly. Grunting then, he went over to the smuggler. "Turn out your pockets."

With mouth tight shut below the snarl of his stare the Mexican sullenly complied. Considering the assortment, Barney picked up the whittled-down pencil, stared a moment at the ornate spurs with their silver chains and danglers. "Put them things back on," he growled, and stood grimly watching while Goyanno did so. "Don't let me catch you paradin' round again without 'em." Then he reached for the wallet, cracking it open to abruptly step back with a broadening grin.

He took out a thick sheaf of currency while the Mexican cursed.

Olds said, "The smugglin' business must be lookin' up. Reckon I won't be needin' no pardners, not with no roll like this in my jeans."

The Mexican ripped out a spate of furious Spanish in which the words 'robber' and 'thief' were thickly interspersed with scurrilous descriptions of someone's ancestry. But Olds only laughed. In high good humor he patiently waited till Goyanno ran out of breath.

"I'm not robbin' anyone," he chuckled. "You weren't asked t' join up with this outfit. You're bein' here's caused considerable unpleasantness — not to mention aggravation, an' the way you've cut in on needed supplies. It's only fair you should pay your way."

The man looked mad enough to burst his surcingle. When he got back enough air to talk with he ungraciously suggested twenty dollars ought to cover any indebtedness he'd incurred.

"I expect that will pay for your grub," Barney nodded. "Let's see," he mused cagily. "Believe you told the colonel this Carmella was your girl, so the vittles she's got away with'll come to another twenty. Then there's charges for haulin' her round an' lookin' after her — that'll be another hundred even," he said, counting it into the pile for himself.

He settled back on his heels to put in a spell of figuring. "We've got to count in the water the two of you have drunk — water's hard t' come by, partic'lar out here at the tag-end of nowhere. Expect that'll chalk up another couple hundred."

He counted some more bills into his pile, looking up to say gravely, "An' there's that rifle of mine you slammed again' a rock — that'll be another hundred. What you got left," he decided with a chuckle, "will just about pay me for the time you've wasted an' the wear an' tear of puttin' up with you."

He held the wallet to an ear and shook it several times before tossing it back to its apoplectic owner. "Sounds like there might still be a few coins in there, but you can have 'em," he said magnanimously, and wheeled away to beckon old Charlie.

XVIII

Having dispatched the Pima with a clean and fully loaded rifle to pack in supplies from Winkelman, Olds spent the rest of the day's brighter hours trying to keep out of the sun and build back some of the strength and energy spent in the miles put behind since quitting Camp Grant.

He fought off sleep with considerable stubbornness but along in mid-morning — jerking out of a trance to find himself nodding and the rifle about to slide off his lap — the precariousness of his situation compelled him to discard his compunctions and deal with the facts.

He could scarcely keep his eyes open — this march had taken more out of him than he'd figured. That was Fact Number One. And Number Two was Goyanno. The smuggler would kill him if he ever got the chance, and Barney dared not put any trust in the girl. The both of them were after his gold — sure, she had saved his bacon with that rock, but she'd been hoping then to wangle a pardnership. Now that that had fallen through it was dollars to doughnuts she'd team up with Goyanno.

Covering him with the rifle Olds ordered the smuggler to get down on his belly and cross both arms behind him. The look this fetched would have scared some folks, but Olds was in too desperately deep already to let mere looks stand in the way of survival. He sent Carmella to get Pammy's halter rope and, when she came back with it, bade her bind Peep's wrists. "Tie him tight," Barney cautioned, "an' don't use up no more of that rope than you have to."

When she stood up, having that thrown rock in mind, he waved her back far enough to make sure it wasn't likely she could bounce a rock off *him.* He then moved in, tested the knots she had tied, took a couple of turns about the smuggler's arms, gruffly told him to get up, marched him across to one of the cottonwoods and tossed the rest of the rope over a low-hanging limb.

Goyanno, by this time, was using some pretty salty language. Olds' cheeks showed the effects of it, turning pink as a scalded lobster; but he went right on with what he was doing and, when the smuggler launched a kick that only narrowly missed connections, jerked all slack from the rope and anchored it securely. "Reckon you'll stay put a while."

Stepping back Olds beckoned the girl. He didn't have any more rope but guessed the reins off the roan would probably keep her snug for three-four hours, which was all he figured to take away from this business. But considering her expressionless cheeks as she came up he was beginning to wonder if he could bring himself to do it. That inscrutably thoughtful turn of her eyes increased his disquiet.

This was nothing, however, to the discomfort he felt when she quietly said, "Don't you think it's about time we drew up those papers?"

He ran the heel of his hand across his unshaven jaw, listening to the gritty scrape of whiskers while she stood there watching, never batting an eye. He had taken it for granted she would know the deal was off when he had shaken down Goyanno, but this apparently had not occurred to her, and he couldn't seem to think of any way to break the news that would not leave him looking like a caught fence crawler.

That was how he felt. Proud as a lost sheepherder, red-faced and squirming with her eyes digging into him and that question still hanging over his head like the side of a mountain about to come down. He had always supposed himself to be the kind that would go down fighting before he would run — and could cite you chapter and verse to prove it — but after the third gulp he backed out of this deadlock lively as a crayfish under full steam.

"Dang if I wasn't just about," he said, "t' chuck that very same notion at you! I got the pencil," he grunted, scooping it up, "but what'll we do fer paper?"

If he'd thought to get out of it on that feeble straw the hope was dashed quickly. Still eyeing him slanchways, she inquired, "What's the matter with the label off one of those tins, the back of it, I mean?"

And that was what they used, Olds perspiringly spelling it out, letter by letter, with Peep's stub of pencil, in laborious scrip. *I, Barney Olds, do hereby give, bequeath and assign forever to Carmella Ramirez a full one-*

half interest in whatever mine, claim —

"Or cache of gold," she said inexorably when Barney, scowling, stopped to wet the pencil.

— *or cache of gold,* he bitterly wrote, *discovered by us jointly* —

"Or by myself alone," she tucked in sweetly, "while hunting for Yuma's chimney on a trip begun at Camp Grant —"

"Hell's fire!" Olds growled. "I can't squeeze in all that!"

"I will get another label —"

"Never mind," he snarled, and cramped it in.

Carmella grinned. "After 'Camp Grant' you'd better put the date — it was the twenty-ninth. And don't forget to sign your name."

He was so riled and disgusted when he got done, he didn't reckon he would sleep a wink. He should have let *her* do the writing. Then it wouldn't have been in his hand. Trouble was she had got him so danged turned around . . .

It was dark when she woke him. She'd got a fire built up, must have slept some herself. The pinched lines didn't show in her face like they had and she'd made some efforts to fix herself up. He bitterly felt the unwanted pull of her.

Goyanno still stood where Olds had tied him and he guessed they had better turn the rat loose and let him get unkinked or they'd be having to feed the son of a bitch with a spoon.

The smell of warming corned beef hovered in the still air, and overhead a scatter of stars was beginning to show and glimmer. He untied the smuggler, watched him collapse on the ground in groaning anguish as the blood began to beat through cramped limbs. But Olds had used up most of his pity and without opening his mouth went back to the fire, helped himself to a plate, and laid out in his mind the long trek still ahead.

Mountain wind crying through the trees swept down off distant unseen heights, and a coyote's yammer came out of the dark beyond the reach of the flickering flames. He felt a lot like that animal wailing out there.

He even thought, rather slowly, of giving up this hunt for Yuma's lost gold, wondering how much real truth there was in it. The samples he'd seen might have come from anyplace. But one thing he knew: they were all of a kind. Increasingly thoughtful, he dug out the piece Carmella had given him. Staring at it he remembered something else and he suddenly looked up, eyes narrowed in astonishment. "By God," he blurted, peering again at the ore, "you got this chunk from the White Horse Bar!"

He saw the flush on her cheeks, the guilty pallor that chased it out of them as she straightened to face him. He glimpsed defiance in that fiercening green stare. "What difference does that make? It belonged to my father — I've more right to it than them!"

"To your father?" Olds growled. "What kinda cock-an'-bull windy is that?"

"He *was* my father!"

"Who was?"

"Yuma!"

Olds stared with dropped jaw. "You must be outa your mind."

It was crazy — preposterous, yet he found himself half convinced already. She was wild enough and conniving enough. Then another thought struck him and he growled, lips curling: "You worked in that dump."

"I sang!" she cried, chin up and eyes furious. "I slept with myself, if that's what you're getting at!"

It was Olds' turn to flush. He threw down his plate and stomped away from the fire, but she sprang after him, hard breathing, to catch and haul him around with a strength that, for her size, seemed about as unlikely as her preposterous claims.

"I am no puta! There was no shame in what I did!"

XIX

They made their next stop some two hours later, alongside a tangle of thorny mesquite where an outcrop of rock pushed up through the grass clumps to provide a bit of shelter from the teeth of the wind.

Goyanno flung himself down in the lee of this ledge while Olds, dismounted, reached to loosen the roan's cinch. "We'll let 'em blow a spell," he grunted as the girl, getting down, floundered over the loose footing to disappear behind the mesquites.

The burro seemed in good enough shape, nuzzling Olds' pockets as he bent over to pick up in turn each of Pammy's neat, well-shod hoofs. Biggest drawback to Carmella, he was sourly reflecting, was her aggravating penchant for having the last word — that and getting her way, whether school-kept or not, were a pair of powerful drawbacks no man considering matrimony was liable to put up with. Not that *he* was leaning that way or even remotely thinking about it but someone, by grab, had ought to set her straight.

He pulled the burro's ears and shook out the blanket after rubbing the cinnamon hide with the dry side, then turned to watch the girl as she came toward him out of the night. She was something to look at, no getting round that. Like a good horse. Shape and style, but ornery and cranky as a basket of snakes. Too smart for her own good, he decided impartially.

"Where are we headed for?" she wanted to know.

"An' bossy," he said under his breath — a combination no man could endure. But now that they were partners — at least on paper — he reckoned she likely had a right to know, so he told her. "Kinda figured," he said, "we might prospect a spell up by Pascual's old stompin' ground. If that's all right with you."

Sarcasm didn't bother her no more than nothing. "There's a shorter way than the one you're taking; save at least five miles. Considering how short we are again on water, I'd say we better take it."

Olds had been opening his mouth to tell her he was quite satisfied with his own way of getting there when mention of the water made him temper the notion. She might just possibly be right. It was when he turned to check, he came to realize, staring, the smuggler was no longer where he'd been beside the rock.

Swearing, he ran over, gun in fist. He went all the way around without catching a glimpse of him, then went around again to make doubly certain.

Carmella, meanwhile, had picked up Charlie's rifle and was peering stiff as a parfleche into the deeper black of the mesquites. Olds, having hit on the selfsame notion, growled: "You take that side, I'll take this."

Working through that tangle was a scratchy job, requiring more time than he liked to think about, and he was sorely tempted to let the smuggler go. More tempted, in fact, than he'd been before, and yet, strangely enough, more reluctant, too, because if that swivel-hipped son suddenly *wanted* to take off — was willing to chance striking off on his own, it would have to be for some reason they weren't going to like.

Carmella, too, seemed to have reached this conclusion; the sounds of her progress told Barney hers was no perfunctory search. Midway through that nightmare of branches Olds got what he figured was a heap smarter notion and, careless of thorns, clawed into the open. Running ahead and around to the far side of this brush, still gripping the pistol he had taken from Goyanno, he took up a stand which would allow him to pounce the moment the quarry was flushed from his covert.

Disappointingly, however, Goyanno didn't show.

He still hadn't been discovered when the girl emerged to stare blankly at Olds. Barney swore in exasperation. It didn't seem possible they both could have missed him but what other explanation would have covered the facts? The fellow must be hiding someplace in the section abandoned when Barney had so abruptly quit the thicket.

Leaving the girl to patrol the surrounding terrain Olds again plunged into that black morass of branches, scouring the overlooked portion with prodigious care, but once more without catching either glimpse or smell of the fox who'd so blithely made fools of the Border Patrol.

Back where they'd started, a good half hour wasted, Olds and the girl exchanged baffled glances. "Do you suppose —" she began, but Olds broke in testily. "If he's still in there I'm a Chinaman's uncle! Hell, he might not ever have gone in there at all. He

— what are you starin' at?"

Olds twisted his head to follow her look and then, coming full around, commenced to swear with a prodigal fury. Goyanno's roan was gone, too!

There wasn't much point in doing any further looking, but when Pammy, peering over a shoulder, began making plaintive sounds of distress, Olds went over to him, muttering, to make an additional bitter discovery. All their water and the last of the beef had joined the smuggler in his hurried departure.

Morning found them in a landscape dominated by rocks, great tumbled mounds of gray weather-cracked stones. The wind had quit and the whole look and feel of the lifeless air was heavy with the promise of another white-hot day.

Olds peered grimly up at Carmella. "Not a cloud in the sky! You still think we'll make it?"

She said through cracked lips, "We've *got* to make it, haven't we?" She swung down off the burro and Pammy grunted his relief. He was showing his age. "I can walk," Carmella declared determinedly. "I can do, or face, anything you can stand up to," and she meant it. "I remember these rocks. . . .

It's probably not over three or four miles now."

She put up a brave show but it seemed to Olds she'd about reached her limit. The lines were back in her cheeks and the prospect of yet another four miles, with the sun boiling down before they'd made two, was enough to discourage even Olds without breakfast.

Some twenty minutes later they came onto the divide and what he saw ahead was even more disheartening than the hunch he'd been nursing. They were higher than he'd figured and the view spread out down there below was cut up worse than a new-sheared sheep, a devil's playground of eroded knobs and gulches and gullies. Even Olds' rock-ribbed courage faltered as he stared down into the jaws of that trap, picturing what it was going to be like by the time that sun got another hour higher. A furnace by comparison would be plush-lined comfort.

The girl must have caught a look at his face. She said: "You aren't about to quit on me now, are you?"

And he'd been worrying about *her!*

Dimples came into the flushed shine of her cheeks and the ghost of her old gamin grin touched her lips. *"Muy malo,"* she said, "but we're not going down there," and set off to the left along the spine of this ridge.

It took some urging to move Pammy again and when, short of patience, Olds was reaching for something to implement his threats he went wide-eyed rigid as his glance chanced to lift across that dark sprawl of canyons and come to grim focus on a faraway knob. There was smoke rising from it, and a second twisting column was coming off the bald scarp of Crozier Peak!

XX

Olds, unutterably weary, was beginning to accept the whirling smoke as mirages of a feverish mind when the girl, after an eternity of stumbling, floundering, fruitless progress, abruptly pulled him to a halt. "Here —" she said in a pixie voice, "drink this," and pressed into his hand the half shell of a gourd.

But when he dipped his face to come at the thing she held back his hand. "Don't gulp it down. You're too hot . . . take it easy."

It didn't taste like much but was wonderously wet and after he had finally gotten it down things quit spinning and, swimming into focus, resolved themselves into an elongated kind of gravelly bench and a white glare of sky.

He must have dozed a while then because the next time he noticed, the sky held the haze of late afternoon, the girl was gone and he was flat on his back half under a bush.

Groaning and grunting he got himself up. So she'd run out on him, had she? Quit him while he was down, left him here like a worn-out boot among the shards of old pots; and he thought, disgustedly, any nump who would look for any different from a woman ought to have his head examined; and rather bitterly swore. "Old pots . . ." he muttered; then it struck him. "Sure! Of course!"

This was Pascual's abandoned camp, the place he had been aiming for. And a dreary sight it was, nothing left but the ground, and it grown over till there wasn't a thing remaining but these scattered fragments of discarded pots. And *where was Pammy!* Had she taken him, too?

Twisting his neck, peering out across this flat, the first thing he noticed was another of them smokes mushrooming in puffs off Brandenburg Mountain, scarcely twelve miles away, and he glared at this evidence of Apache persistence, clawed by a clamor of sharpening worries. Then he spotted another, nearer even than that, and found a third hazily hanging over Antelope Peak, which was plumb around in the opposite direction; and when he saw the fourth coming off the Black Hills he knew they had him ringed.

He didn't hear Carmella until she was practically on top of him; then, besides being startled, his confusion was confounded by the sight of a brace of rabbits she was dangling by the ears.

She handed him his rifle, said she was glad to see him up, and all he could do was gawp like a fool. It wasn't so much her having bagged those jacks as that she'd found the strength to look for them even; and he was further flabbergasted that she'd bothered to come back.

He finally blurted, still staring: "I don't believe, by God, you're *real!*"

Her green, watching eyes, in the quick look she gave him, seemed to Olds a little queer. "Oh, I'm real enough." She said, rather shortly: "Come on. We're camped down below —"

"But I should think, by grab . . . all that walkin' —"

"I didn't have to go far."

"But after las' night an' that hike this mornin' —"

"That was yesterday. This is Pascual's old camp. I've scarcely walked a hundred yards since we got here."

Barney couldn't believe it.

"Don't you remember me feeding you?" She smiled up to him shyly. "Holding your head while you drank?"

Olds, flushing, continued to scowl.

"I've spoon-fed you five times." Her laugh sprang free, sweet and excited as some mate-minded mockingbird. "You don't remember coming up here? 'Just for a look' was what you said; but when I came up to see what was keeping you, there you were, stretched out and snoring —"

"Hell's fire!" Olds cried fiercely. "Ain't you seen them smokes?"

She looked and nodded, curiously watching him. "What have smokes got to do with it?"

"Got to — God all mighty! Don't you know them Injuns'll —"

"Those aren't Apache smokes."

Olds stared, mouth open.

She said, "I can read Apache smoke." And then, to his blank, stupid look: "I can't make anything of that."

Olds twisted his head. "By Gawd, you're right! That's Morse," he mumbled — "telegrapher's talk . . ." and his lips skinned back in the snarl of a wolf as the implications dropped into the cold lump of his stomach.

"Feltenmeyer's patrols!" he cursed.

"But don't you see? They can't bother you now that we're partners."

Before he could speak, the sound of approaching hoofbeats pulled both of them around. Olds, alarmed, was reaching for the rifle when Charlie came into sight atop the crest of a distant ridge. Two horses, on lead, were presently followed by a couple of animals heavy-laden with packs. Olds looked again to make sure.

"In the morning," he said with considerable satisfaction, "we'll go look fer that chimney," and found her staring so strangely he whirled to peer across her shoulder. Discovering no alarming circumstance, he grumbled, "What's the matter?"

With a queer, half scornful laugh the girl said: "It was the Arivaipas, not Pascual, who had that gold."

Olds, bristling, scrubbed at his scraggle of whiskers. "Well, sure, but —"

"The place *they* were camped is northeast of here — a long, hard ride. At least *two days* if we're going to pack in."

XXI

It was one of the mighty few times in a vociferous life Barney Olds had been caught

155

without appropriate comeback. But she was right. Right as rain! Pascual couldn't have told gold from sour apples!

Grabbing up his rifle, too impatient to stand still, Olds set off to meet his Indian henchman. And the girl, tightly clamping determined lips, set off after him.

Time he met up with Charlie he had a pretty fair lead, and the way it boiled down it was a good thing he had because, politeness out of the way, the first thing the old grave-robber said was: "Where's Charlie's squaw?"

Barney's cheeks went white, then dark with embarrassed anger. "We'll talk about that later," he gruffed. "You git everythin' I sent you fer?"

The Pima waved a sullen hand; his mean yellow eyes began to roll. "You ketch whiskey?"

"Not yet," Olds said, "but you'll git it, don't worry . . . when we find that chimney."

Charlie's head reared up on the stringy old neck and the wrinkled old mouth pulled back off his teeth. "Yes!" he grunted after a long, dead-eyed silence. "Me wait. You give Charlie squaw now."

Olds could hear the girl coming up. He hadn't the time nor the tolerance for any more haggling, and growled sharp and

short: "You'll git your squaw when *I* say —
that plain enough?"

The old buck's hands tightened round
Goyanno's rifle, but with Barney's repeater
looking him square in the eye about all he
could do was take it. He showed mighty
poor grace with his eyes like peeled grapes,
the whole length of him trembling but,
banging his heels against the paint's ribs, he
finally moved off without further comment.

Letting go of held breath Olds fell in
behind, the pack mules following, knowing
in his bones he wasn't done with this yet.
He said nothing at all when the girl, looking
curious, swung in beside him. But Carmella
said thinly: "What was that all about?"

Barney's scowl blackly tightened. He said,
"Don't bother me now," and plowed right
along. When they came up to the small,
careful fire she had built Olds, stabbing a
glance at the downheeling sun, stamped the
coals into the shale and kicked dirt over
them. "We're goin' t' push right on," he
growled over a shoulder. And, going to the
mules, began to paw through the packs.

Finally satisfied, he relashed the loads,
somewhat dubiously eyeing the waterbags.
They were damp and bulging but he wished
they had more just to be on the safe side. It
was while he was thinking this, still scowl-

ing, that he remembered something else, and came around, stare sharpening. "Thought I told you," he said, "t' git *horses!*"

Charlie was scornful. "Heap better mules. More tougher!"

And he was right about that. But Olds had a right to look suspicious. There hadn't been enough money for the purchase of mules. Barney pointed this out.

The old reprobate grinned. "Me stealum!"

A fine kettle of fish! Barney felt like knocking the Indian down. There was trouble enough without stealing mules and bringing the civil law into this, too. "You nizzy old fool," he snarled, flushed with anger. "Don't you know it'll be reported?"

"No report," Charlie chuckled. "Me killum!"

Barney threw up his hands. It was no good explaining to this half-baked old savage that you couldn't kill the law — be nothing but a goddam waste of breath. This was what a man got for tying up with an Injun! Seemed like nothing he did ever turned out right. He was stuck with it now, and with whatever came out of it — same way he was stuck with this dadblamed girl! About all he could do was make sure Charlie didn't . . .

And then Barney swore. There was *noth-*

ing he could do. That crazy damn Injun had a cartridge belt strapped round him, and every loop was filled!

Charlie's look was bad. And when he saw the direction of his white brother's stare he laughed his wild cackle and brandished the rifle in a show of fierce challenge. "El Mocho keep treaty or me killum squaw!"

They quit Pascual's campsite an hour short of sundown, all of them mounted and no one inclined to run off at the mouth. Talk, Barney knew, wasn't going to solve a thing. The only chance he could see now was to latch onto that chimney. Gold could find an answer to pretty near anything. He looked bitterly reckless, scarcely less fierce than old Charlie himself; and the mood was still on him when the Pima threw a hand up, silently pointing.

They were an hour out of camp and Olds had reasonably figured if they'd anything to fear from Peep Goyanno the danger would be there, for the smuggler knew that to have been their destination. But facts were facts, and what he saw now was a dark bunched clot of traveling dots that were obviously horsemen and plainly not moving in any military manner.

These were perhaps two miles out and

palpably bent on closing with Olds' party. Even as he watched it became increasingly apparent, as the group thinned and spread, whoever was in charge grimly meant to intercept him.

Olds slanched a look at Charlie and — in that moment — was glad to have a fighting man handy. But any guile the Pima had developed or inherited had evidently left him when he became the recipient of a white man's gun. Fight, was his answer to everything. "Me killum!" he grinned, and was lifting his weapon when Olds grabbed the barrel.

He said, "It may come t' that, but the feller that gits away will have a lot better chance —"

"I think I can get us away," spoke up Carmella, cutting in; and, turning her back on that line of black dots, put the horse under her into a run. This wasn't exactly what Barney'd had in mind, but there was nothing left now but to take out after her. The Indian didn't appear to care much for it either. Olds had to pretty near yell himself hoarse to get the fool even to look in his direction. He was more trouble really than them stubborn dang mules. But they were finally strung out in the wake of the vanishing girl.

Dropping over the rim of a water-cut wash Barney saw her ahead of them, pounding east through the hock deep sand of its bed. But a hundred yards later, peering ahead through the gloom, he began to get hold of what the girl had in mind. Though he still didn't like it he had to admit it made sense.

They were going steeply down a shale-ragged spur that let into those badlands they had skirted coming up here. If they were to shake that bunch this was certainly the place to do it. A feller could sure get turned around quick down there. They'd be almighty lucky not to get turned around themselves!

Just the same Olds wasn't too comfortable about it, finding himself pounding after Carmella in a whirling welter of mismatched notions. Seemed like he'd ought to have stood pat with old Charlie. Even faced with such odds — and there must have been upwards of two dozen of them back there! He felt like running demeaned him someway, sort of put a man's courage in question.

Still, the Apache way of thinking had considerable to commend it. They wasn't never fussed or worried about appearances. They was strong for big odds and when things went against them they believed in

161

leaving pronto, living to fight another day. Sure as hell he wouldn't latch onto any gold back there!

"You know where you're goin'?" he called to the girl.

He didn't know if she heard him, what with all this racket. If she made any answer it was drowned in the wild rataplan of hoofs thrown back off the rocks, regurgitating like thunder. In all that uproar he couldn't tell if those fellers were after them or not.

The same thought finally must have come to the girl. She stopped so short a pile-up was only narrowly averted. *"Listen!"* she cried with her horse hauled around sideways; and they all sat like statues while the echoes fell away.

If there was pursuit — and Barney would have bet his bottom dollar on the likelihood — the pursuers must also have come to a standstill, for nothing came out of the windy dark.

Keeping his voice down Olds gruffly said: "You know where we're at? Think you can git us outa here?"

She appeared to be thinking. There was no chance of making out her face in this gloom for it was blacker down here than a stack of damned stovelids. But it seemed like to Barney — regardless of her words —

she was a long way from confident. "I was *born* in this country," she said, kind of huffy. "I've been all through these gullies."

"Yeah, but how long ago?"

"Not so long I can't find my way out!"

Olds hoped she wasn't just wishing. "Go ahead then," he growled. "There's a whole heap of places I'd a sight rather be than down in this jumble when the sun gits up." Scowling round him he said: "Maybe you know where that gold's at, too, huh?"

He glimpsed the regretful shake of her head. "But I can take you to where the Arivaipas were camped. When we get out of here it's almost straight north."

"What are we waitin' fer?"

"If you don't want to hoof it we'd better blow these horses."

So they sat where they were for another ten minutes, all of them listening into the wind. The quiet of this place without movement was about on a par with the caverns of the moon, or like Calabasas after the hotel had gone up in smoke. It was uncanny and worrisome, the more so since Olds was taking no stock in the possibility of those jaspers he'd seen having abandoned whatever they'd been trying to bring off. They were back there someplace — he could feel it in his bones.

When he got all he could take of this cat-and-mouse business he blew out his cheeks and told the girl to push on. There were times when a man would sooner be a dead hero than put up with the pressures that went with staying alive.

Sometime after midnight they stopped again to rest their animals, and it was just as quiet there as it had been back yonder. "I think we've lost them," Carmella whispered but Olds found himself unable to buy this. His luck wasn't running that way and he knew it. Still hoping, however, he put it up to the Indian.

Charlie grunted. "Mebbeso go round rim," he offered discouragingly, and the more Olds considered this the more likely it seemed. Some of them, certainly, might well have done this; others could be dogging their trail to make sure. Goyanno was cunning enough to have hit on such a strategem.

Twice Carmella threw him into cursing tantrums when it seemed she had someway taken a wrong fork. The first time she hadn't — it was nothing but a miscalculation of distance between the last turn and the cut she was looking for. The second time, though, it took five struck matches — Olds more jumpy with each fresh flare — before she got her bearings, and even then looked so dubious he almost struck her. "What the hell kinda reed are we leanin' on, anyway? You're supposed t' *know!*" he said, tearing into her. "By grab," he snarled, "if you've gone an' got us lost —"

"If you can do any better," she came back at him bitterly, "go ahead and do it!" and glared, chin up, looking about ready to walk off and leave him.

Perhaps it shook a little sense into Olds. At least it silenced him.

She drew a hand across her cheeks, still stiff with defiance. "We're not lost," she said at last. "We've come out of our way perhaps two miles. We can backtrack if you want, but this trail will fetch us out if we stay with it. It's up to you."

Olds waved her on, not trusting himself to speak.

XXII

In the leaden gray cold of a cheerless false dawn they appeared to be scarcely more than half a mile from the ghostly north rim. Olds scrubbed his eyes, hardly able to believe it. But it was lighter up there and the ragged line of cliffs could not be mistaken for anything else against the brightening sky. Relief loosened his muscles and a kind of grudging acknowledgement of Carmella's achievement put a twist of grin across his beard-stubbly jaws.

But the girl wasn't looking. All her attention appeared to be focused on the crags farther west where a notch in the rimrocks suggested a pass. She said, pointing: "There's the place I expected to come out. But we've not lost much, except some easier going, because the Ari—"

"Mens up there!" exclaimed the Indian, cutting into her talk with a sudden excitement. Though Olds saw no movement he was willing to believe, herding them all behind the cover of some rocks. "What was they up to?" he wanted to know. By Charlie's tell they'd been watching the trail — the other one; and that figured. Like enough they'd fixed up an ambush, Olds told himself, and if she hadn't got them lost he might be laid out by this time, ready for planting. It wasn't too joyful a thought even for him, but there it was. The dratted girl had saved his life!

It looked a terrible burden to find yourself under, and if there'd been any whiskey he'd have joined Charlie in it. Since there wasn't he did his best to keep a stiff upper lip and get his mind fixed on something less harrowing to contemplate, like what could be done if that bunch up there spotted them.

If things really got sticky he guessed Charlie could be depended on to thin them out a little. The nizzy old coot would sooner kill than eat, Barney reckoned disgustedly, and was figuring to keep a close watch on the redskin when Carmella, twisting round, thrust her face up close to his.

"I don't know how we'll get past," she said, "without them seeing us."

Olds, frowning, considered. "What's up top of that rim?"

"Mostly open country."

"How far?"

"Three or four miles."

She was so close he could feel the flutter of her breath and he drew back, suddenly nervous till he saw how upset she was and worried. That strengthened him someway. He patted her shoulder. "You done good, for a woman. Real good," he said magnanimously. "I'll git us outa this. Don't you fret."

She gave him a queer look which he might have found unsettling had his attention not been too taken up to notice. "What's the matter," he said, "with layin' low fer a bit? Them jaspers up yonder, if we keep outa sight, will git t' stewin' an' fumin' afore the day gits much older. Might git so worked up when nobody shows they'll slip down off them bluffs figurin' t' dig us out."

He gave Charlie a hand sign and, getting out of his saddle, watched the others follow suit. With the animals on short rein they cautiously made their way deeper into the rocks which had come down off the cliffs. The girl stayed close to Olds but the boulder Charlie picked to hunker behind was farther removed than Barney would have countenanced had there been no risk to raising his voice.

The first hour passed, not enjoyably but finally. Every little while they had to change their positions to get the benefit of what little shade there was. The temperature down in this windless pocket continued to climb, as did Barney's impatience. He couldn't make out the pass from where he was squatted, nor could the girl, but he guessed any change would not escape Cheek Creek Charlie who had his head in a bush halfway up a rubbled slide.

A disturbing notion got to wriggling around at the back of his head, but before he could give it any proper notice the horses began to display signs of restiveness, alarmingly stamping and shaking their heads. Probably anxious for water, but all the water was on the mules and Olds was reluctant to make any move which might attract the attention of that bunch at the pass.

He peered at the Indian, still as a log on that rubble of rotten rock.

Infected by the horses the mules began to shift around under their loads and Barney, disgruntledly eyeing that waggling of ears, knew in his bones he'd better see to them pronto before they gave voice to their discontent. One hee-haw in the deep well of this silence could touch off more than he was ready to cope with — and it could be just as bad if they got out from under the cover of these rocks.

He went cautiously forward, striving to keep himself out of sight of anyone happening to look from the pass. Just as he was reaching for the nearest mule and the pair of waterbags damply resting against the bulge of its pack, he caught the unmistakable clop of shod hoofs.

Olds, shocked stiff, stood frozen in midstride, one boot still lifted, while the implications of that sound banged through him. Teeth bared, he twisted his head for a look which discovered no more than he had already noticed. Nothing new met his glance yet the sounds were still audible, sometimes muted, more often plain, certainly growing more ominously loud and obviously originating in the gulch they'd come out of to get where they were.

He was filled with a confusion that was almost panic, wondering how much time they might have, knowing it was bound to be measured in seconds, that there wouldn't be enough to negotiate the cliffs before whoever it was disastrously hove into sight. Knowing he'd no time to muzzle these animals, understanding that they were irrevocably trapped.

The girl's ashen cheeks showed that she knew, too. And, even as realization of all this struck him, the off-mule lustily announced their presence with a gate-hinge bray.

Thrown back from the rocks, that sound was like a clarion.

Strangely, suddenly cool as a well chain, Olds lowered his foot and lifted his rifle with a twisted grin. But it was kill-crazy Charlie who got off the first shot.

Three riders, emerging from the gulch behind them, were stopped cold with shock by the Indian's yell. Olds' rifle spoke and the foremost rider pitched out of his saddle in a headlong fall. Charlie's piece kept pounding and the second man wilted but the third, shouting hoarsely, wheeled his mount and spurred from sight, leaving Olds, goggle-eyed, too astounded to close his mouth.

The girl yelled, "What's the matter?" and her eyes looked big as slop buckets in a face stretched thin with fright. Olds peered at her unseeingly. "Are you *hit?*" she cried, running recklessly toward him.

"I'm all right," he growled. "Git back an' stay down. It's just that — Hell," he said, "you better hev this gun," and passed her the six-shooter he'd taken from Goyanno.

He still looked like a man half asleep. "What is it?" she insisted, only partially reassured.

"That third guy," he said. "Did you git a look at him?"

She shook her head and put an arm out to touch him. "I'm all right," he grumbled, and pawed at his face with the handless arm as though he were trying to scrape cobwebs off it. "That buck that got away just now — that was *Fek Shinnan,* Sully's top scout an' a bad guy t' cross. Sully — George Sullivan," he said to her blank look. "The grubstake king!" he said savagely, and cursed.

It was plain his words made no sense at all to her.

"Look —" he growled, still with his stare on the angle of wall behind the dropped pair where Shinnan had disappeared, "Sully's been keepin' me in grub over most of five years. These grubstakes of his was each one of 'em dated; whatever I struck inside of that date he got half of. Trouble was I never turned up a thing. So a couple weeks back he put a piece in the papers he was no longer liable fer any bills I run up — washed his hands of me, see? *Now,*" he snarled through a fresh spate of cursing, "here's Fek Shinnan camped on my tail with a bunch of blood-hungry gunnies!

"You don't git it?" he cried, looking back at her, disgusted. "Means he's teamed up with Goyanno — it's got to! Nobody but Peep could hev any idea we're on the trail of that chimney — that sonuvabitch Peep heard us jawin' about it an' run straight t' George!"

"But how could he?" she said. "He's alone in the desert —"

"All that believe that kin stand on their heads! I dunno how he done it, but he got hold of George someway — it was *their* smokes we seen! I shoulda guessed that ol' buzzard would be in at the kill! Prob'ly got his whole crew here!"

Her eyes were dark wells behind the scared cheeks; and then her whole look changed with excitement, and she cried, grabbing hold of him: "There's another way out — we don't *have* to go up that wall."

Olds stared. "Another way . . . ?" And Charlie, springing pantherlike out of the rocks, nodding, grunted: "Tres Piñons!" The grip of her eyes held Barney like a gun. "Yes! the Tres Piñons trail! It's out of the way — maybe ten miles farther, but —"

"Hell!" Olds cried impatiently. "What're we waitin' on? Git whackin', girl!" and gave her a shove in the direction of her horse. "Let's git movin' 'fore that bunch up top comes swarmin' down on us!"

And, with Charlie whooping like a pulque-drunk Apache, the exodus was on. Several slugs whistled round them as they sprang to horse but no one was hit and almost before you could mutter Jo Jinkens they were all astride and larruping their mounts through the house-sized boulders and lining them out on a brush grown trail that turned and twisted like a broken-backed snake.

They'd be followed, all right — Olds had no doubt of that, but anything looked better than being penned up in that rock-ribbed pocket, caught in the crossfire Goyanno had set up for them with Sullivan's help.

It was deeply dark, not a star in sight, when Carmella — riding point — called back, "This is it."

XXIII

The Indian shook him awake at first light. Barney, hacking and spitting, got up and looked around, seeking the ridge and, considerably astonished, discovering the greasewood stubbled spine of a low hogback off yonder which appeared to be headed in the right direction. Considerably encouraged despite the pessimism experience had ground into him, Olds picked up his rifle and, without pausing to eat or wake Carmella who was still in her blankets, set off with Charlie to have a look at the terrain.

What he'd glimpsed could certainly have passed for a ridge in this country. Mesquite, in the middle distance, prevented him from forming any reasonable estimate of the promontory's length, but it appeared to stretch away for at least several miles, and this was in line with what Olds had heard.

It suddenly occurred to him as peculiar he hadn't thought to go over this region before. He hadn't come this far north in his prospecting. Had been put off, he reckoned, by the same miscalculation which had misled the soldiers who had found Crittenden's horse. The basin he'd been over so fruitlessly and frequent must, Olds suspected, be just east and somewhat south of this range of tumbled hills.

At least the girl had given him a new perspective. Anxious to get started Barney, the Pima following, headed back to camp. This was still a good half hour short of sunup and the night's lingering chill made the notion of a breakfast fire uncommonly hard to resist.

When they got back to the camp Carmella's blankets were thrown back and empty. She was nowhere in sight. Probably gone off to find some privacy, Olds reckoned and, going over to the packs, got out his skinning knife and began opening cans of bully. Wouldn't be what King George would be sitting down to but at least it would stick to their ribs for a while. He wasn't about to light no fires — not with Fek Shinnan out bending the grass!

When ten minutes dragged past, still without any sign of the girl, Olds began to look uneasy. He checked the animals — all there. He finally said to Charlie in a worried kind of voice: "You know where that spring is?"

The Pima looked at him blankly, shaking his head.

"She can't hev gone far. See if you can pick out her tracks."

The Indian, bent over, loped around in two circles, then grunting set off like a hound after a fox, mumbling and muttering as he nosed out the trail. Down off the bench they went, off into the west toward a jumble of rocks out of which grew a tangle of ironwood and catclaw.

At one point the Indian stopped to look up, shading his eyes beneath the flat of a hand. Grunting, he set off again, Barney crowding his heels. They weren't twenty jumps from that collection of boulders when a terrified scream froze old Charlie in mid-stride.

Olds went over that gound like a giraffe, bounding into those rocks like he'd been flung from a catapult. What he saw was enough to freeze a man's blood. Carmella, with her clothes clutched against the front of her, eyes big as saucers in that pinched white face, was backed against the flat of a barn-sized boulder just across the pool. Fangs gleaming, a snarling cougar was just leaving another in a spread-clawed leap.

There wasn't even time to get the rifle to his shoulder. Olds fired from the hip. The big cat dropped in mid-flight, falling into the pool still spitting and clawing, not three feet from the girl. Carmella crumpled.

Barney's own knees felt pretty weak, but

he got over there.

He had no recollection of snatching her up, wet hair, bare skin, yielding curves and all. When he came to himself she was clamped right to him, soaked head boring into his shoulder, trembling and shaking, bawling like a heifer, him with both arms round her and, off at the other side of the pool, Cheek Creek Charlie staring like a goon.

Olds growled, red-faced, "Go fetch a horse here, Injun!"

The Pima's look was hard to figure, compounded as it was of so many jangling emotions, but he whirled and took off when Barney, swearing, made a dive for his rifle. That bugger was getting too big for his britches, like as if Olds hadn't enough worries already.

The girl had her clothes on when Olds turned back, and appeared to have gotten over the worst of her fright. Her eyes were still red, her cheeks splotched with tears, but the smile she had for him should have melted even the heart of a bartender, such pure thankfulness was in it, such adoration and trust. "I never felt so unstrung in my life," she said earnestly. "I don't know *what* I'd have done if you hadn't —"

"What happened to that pistol I give you?"

She shook her head. "In my blankets I guess."

"Well, you better make a habit of keepin' it on you. Better keep a eye on that Injun, too. I don't like the way he's been lookin' at you."

"Oh, I will," she assured him, then smiled again shyly. "But he won't do anything long's *you*'re around."

Olds, scowling, said hurriedly, "Don't you reckon we better sashay back t' camp? I just opened up some beef. We don't want that redskin gobblin' — that guy's a reg'lar goat. Eat anythin' he kin git his dang choppers on!"

He thought her look a mite odd; but she did not object when, scooping up his rifle, he took hold of her arm to help her out of the rocks. If she put more of her weight on him than she needed to he stood up under it manfully without complaint.

By the time they'd all eaten, repacked the mules and put their gear on the horses, the sun was beginning to really bear down. Olds had thought some of leaving the camp where it was in the proximity of water, but the memory of Fek Shinnan had decided him against it. Better to keep everything in one lump, and in country like this the farther they stayed from waterholes the more likely it appeared they might live to drink another day. And he wasn't just thinking about mountain lions either!

Some things seen were hard to put from mind and not infrequently Olds' glance would covertly shift toward the younger of his partners, these occasions being marked by a rise in color before some inner turmoil made him snatch his look away.

The ridge continued through mesquite and huisache clumps to drift generally in a northerly direction. When he reckoned they had covered approximately three miles, the line of hills he'd been studying didn't hardly seem more than a couple of whoops away.

And they sure looked rough enough. Great mounds of ribbed-up rock left stark and bare where the winds of countless eons had scoured them till mighty little remained of their original estate, a few gnarled cedars and the tortured shapes of half-dead juniper bravely flaunting among the rust reds and scabrous yellows and occasional stippling of mottled green.

Still following the ridge, which now appeared to be a spur of this deteriorated range, Olds and his partners pressed steadily north for another five or six miles with everything thus far appearing in line with what he had heard about the chimney's location.

Filled with an expanding exuberance, Olds could hardly contain himself. He wanted to shout and jump around, suddenly deciding in the whirl of this excitement to leave the animals and press on afoot lest, in their impatience to pinpoint the treasure, they pass it by without ever knowing.

"We'll camp down there," he told Charlie, pointing out a pocket some hundred yards to the left. The Indian, expressionless but still gripping his rifle, led their single file departure off the side of the spur. The place was a veritable oven of trapped heat, but Olds in his dither cared nothing for that — he wasn't proposing to stay in camp. All their waterbags were filled. Carmella had seen to that before rolling into her blankets last night.

When they got down onto this baking flat Barney delegated all the chores to Charlie. "An' don't fergit t' give these critters some water," he admonished the inscrutable Pima. "We're not goin' a great ways — oughta be back by nosebag time, but keep your eyes peeled an' watch out fer snakes."

Taking nothing but the pick and his Henry repeater Olds, with a final, hurried look around, passed Carmella a water bag. Then, remembering they might need a shovel, he dug that out for the girl to carry, too. With her following, squaw fashion, Barney led off.

The next two hours, he confidently expected, should settle this business one way or the other. He knew he'd always been destined to find Yuma's gold. Olds had suddenly become so certain of this he'd even debated for a moment leaving the girl behind. And he still didn't know quite why he hadn't.

Just beyond the flat where they'd left Charlie and the packs they came upon the gulch he had noticed from the ridgetop. It lay about right to fit in with the stories. They worked along the south side of it, forcing their way through a tangle of brush. This was hot, sweaty work but in Olds' present state he scarcely noticed. The girl dropped back to avoid slapping branches although she, by this time, was pretty jumpy herself. "If we went a little higher," she suggested presently, "we'd be out of this brush. Didn't Crittenden say they kept well up from the bottom?"

Barney scowled. The freighter had, for a fact. Thus reminded, Olds scrambled into a more commanding position and, not waiting for the girl, began to move east across the scabrous slope, eyes on the lookout for any craterlike depression which might serve to mask the top of Yuma's chimney.

Of course the place by now might be grown over. A man had to keep his wits about him. With the sun beating down from almost straight up this was grueling work, so much so that presently even Olds was forced to pause long enough to catch second wind. One thing was sure — if the gold was here it wasn't far away.

They had gone perhaps a mile along the flank of this gulch when the girl suggested, during one of Olds' stops, it was possible what they were looking for might be on the other slope. "Yeah," Barney grumbled, "I been thinkin' about that."

Catching up his pick and rifle he started down the slope. Tearing a course through the brush he scrambled up the other side but had not gone far when the girl let out a shout. Peering back, alarmed and irritated too, he saw her throw up a hand, begin waving it wildly. He started to yell, thought better of the notion and, swearing, went back to learn the cause of her excitement.

"Look at this!" she cried as he emerged from the clutch of that thorny tangle, and tossed whatever it was she had hold of. Olds caught it and stared, snorting with contempt. "Hell's fire!" he swore, "that's nothin' but pyrites — fool's gold," he snarled, pitching it away in disgust.

"Well . . . it *looked* like gold, all glittery and . . . *What's that!*"

With Fek Shinnan and Goyanno never wholly out of mind the startled pitch of her voice yanked Olds around, eyes white ringed as a stallion bronc's. Back snicked the hammer of his lifting rifle as, following her stare, he caught the flicker of movement.

XXIV

Finger whitening against the trigger, Olds was all set to fire when out of a scriggle of brush stepped a breech-clouted shape, smokepole in one hand, the other raised in the 'peace' sign.

Olds' face darkened angrily. "Thought I told you t' stay with the stock!"

Cheek Creek Charlie drew himself up grandly. "Me pardner! Where El Mocho go, Charlie go!"

"A fine kettle of fish!" Barney blew out his cheeks in frustrated impotence. Half minded to shoot the old bastard and be done with it, he looked sure enough fit to burst his surcingle. "What about them horses?"

"Horses hobbled!"

"What about them packs?"

"Me hide!"

Olds, though still plenty riled, was too impatient to get on with the hunt to waste further time on the nizzy old coot. With a wave of his handless arm he motioned to the top of the slope. "Git up there an' keep your eyes peeled — savvy? Anyone comes you let me know. *And,*" he tacked onto it, glaring fiercely, "you do what I say or there'll be another redskin bitin' the dust. Now git at it!"

Carmella, when he peered around for her, was picking her way through the thorns down below. "Where you off to?" he growled after her.

"If it was on that side we should have found it by now."

"It's *got* t' be here!" Olds declared, and kept looking.

This was thirsty work with that sun beating down, but the girl had their water sack and he was too proud to let her know the inside of him felt drier than a bale of ten-year-old cotton — and too stubborn to go over there.

Wiping sweat from his face Olds abruptly bent down, narrowly staring at a shallow sunken place he'd almost missed so nearly covered was the depression with the pale spiked pads of pear. Batting these aside with the flat of his pick, he put down his rifle and gingerly scooped out a handful of dirt. It was powdered like flour and, with pounding heart, he jumped to his feet. Catching up the pick by its hickory haft he sunk the head of it with one mighty swing.

All that was covered by that loose-feeling dirt was an Indian fire pit. He glared at it, whipped, too disgusted to swear.

"Come here," Carmella called while he was mopping his face, and he looked over at her, scowling. Another chunk of pyrites, probably. But there was nothing over here worth the waste of further time. He picked up his rifle.

"What is it?" he said, puffing, when he finally got over there. She was bent over a kind of hollow, scooping out dirt with the shovel. "Wait — don't tell me," he grumbled, "let me guess. Fire pit, ain't it?"

"I don't know," she said. "I stumbled over those rocks and when I saw what they were this seemed a good place to dig." She straightened up and stepped back. "You want to try with that pick?"

Olds was peering at the rocks. These outlined roughly half of what appeared to have been a sort of raggedy circle, carefully fitted as for the coping of a well. Excited again, Olds stepped round the girl. The place where she had been using the shovel was just inside that border of stones and appeared somewhat lower than the ground outside.

Considering the rocks again Olds reckoned the circle, had it been complete, would have been about six feet in diameter, which certainly agreed with Crittenden's description of the excavation from which he and Yuma had taken their samples. Suddenly trembling, Olds wiped the palm of his hand against his thigh and, stepping off six feet from that half-moon of rocks, sank his pick. It went in three inches and, clanging, jumped from his hand.

He said: "Gimme that shovel!"

Scraping away the dirt he brought other rocks to sight, stones fitted precisely and in the same arrangement as the wind-exposed half circle which had caught Carmella's attention. Dropping into the shallow hole Olds took up the pick and got busy in earnest. When he stepped back to rest the girl cleared the loose stuff away with the shovel. They were three feet down and both breathing hard when the pick went grating into something more resistant than earth. "Oh!" the girl cried. "What is it, Barney?"

Olds reached for the shovel but he was

shaking so hard he had to sit down. "I'll do it," Carmella said, and cleared away the loosened earth.

They were considerably chagrined and no little let down when she dug from the clods nothing more stimulating than a bent and rusted tobacco tin with a hole near one end where the pick had gone in.

It was a stupendous disappointment, keyed up as they had been. Barney's shoulders sagged. He looked terribly discouraged — even Carmella appeared ready to quit.

She tossed the thing aside, lips tight. Then, suddenly blinking, went after it, whacking it impatiently against the shovel's side until the rust-eaten metal of the lid fell apart, disclosing two edges of a folded paper.

Their glances met and clung. Olds said with a shrug, "They always put in paper liners —"

"But this hasn't any foil. It's been peeled off!"

Barney stiffened. Grabbing it out of her hand he flicked it open, spread it against his knee. The watching girl saw his face turn gray.

"What is it?" she cried. And Barney, all of a tremble again and still with that strange glazed look to his eyes, held it out. There was writing on the paper. A pencil had scrawled: 23rd October, 1860. *McLean and Crittenden.*

Still with that disbelieving look on his jowls Olds dropped back into the hole and, clearing away the loose earth, tackled the project again with the pick. The girl looked puzzled. "Crittenden was Yuma's partner. But who was this McLean?"

"Thomas F.," Olds grunted between swings. "Better knowed at the Academy as 'Buffalo Tom.' The cashiered looey — Yuma himself."

Gasping, Carmella said, "My father . . ."

"Come off it," Olds said, "he was no more your father than I am."

She looked at him slanchways, resentful, defensive.

Olds leaned on the pick handle. "Hell, it makes no diff'rence t' me," he said bluntly, "but that guy was dead long before you was born!"

A flush drove the paleness out of her cheeks. "How can *you* know!"

"I kin add two an' two. The last trip McLean took was the same year as that paper — 1860. His Injun wife went with him and the Papagoes beat them to death with clubs. They never had no children — they never had time."

He went back to his half-hearted picking. On the fourth swing the point of his pick slapped into something *ker-chunk.* And when he tried to disengage it for another whack, whatever he'd got into didn't want to let go.

First he tried to scoop the dirt away with his hand. With sudden impatience he snatched up the shovel. He was the best one-handed worker the girl had ever seen. It didn't take long to find what he was into. In astounded exuberance he let go with a shout. In the flush of excitement Carmella joined him. "What is it?" she asked, crowding curiously against him, trying to see across his shoulder.

With the earth clinging to it the rock that held his pick seemed to Carmella less of a discovery than the rusty tin can she'd found, until Barney, running his thumb across a blaze the shovel had left, said: "Gold — *by God we've found it!*"

When he got his pick pried out of its grip even she, staring into the glint of that wound, could see it was the same kind of ore as the sample she'd stolen from the White Horse Bar. "You mean," she exclaimed, "we've found Yuma's Chimney?"

Barney jumped from the hole and danced her around. "That's just what we've done!"

In the midst of these gyrations the stump of Olds' bad arm began to give him fits, as it always did when a storm was making up — just as it had the night they'd left Camp Grant. He twisted his neck for a squint at the sky and was surprised to see how far down the sun had got, but he couldn't find anything wrong with the look of it. There wasn't a cloud in sight.

"Well," he growled, peering into their excavation, "I s'pose we ought t' fill this in. Kinda seems a shame, but we sure wouldn't want someone else latchin' onto it." He commenced scuffing the dirt with one of his mangy looking boots. "Here — you take the shovel. . . . You're mighty quiet — anythin' wrong?"

She'd been staring, darkly thoughtful. Now she said with a frown, "You were right about Yuma not being my father — I've told some awful whoppers. I don't deserve all this. . . ." She waved a hand at the hole.

"You ain't gittin' all of it. Only your half," Olds threw back with a chuckle. Still flushed with the magnitude of their wonderfully good luck, crammed with all the confident assurance and roseate visions engendered by this astounding achievement where so many before them had so miserably failed, he said in the comfort of his tumultuous feelings, "There ain't no one I'd rather have fer a pardner. Fer sheer pluck an' stamina — hell!"

Letting go of the shovel, not able more adequately to express the tremendous excitement inside him, he caught the girl to him, wrapping both arms around her, and kissed her soundly square on the mouth.

They were both astonished, Olds so much so that, tightening his grip, he did it again.

When they stepped back, shaken, Olds ludicrously grinning and both of them staring as though they'd never before caught a look at each other, it was Carmella, flushed and radiant, who snatched up the shovel and vigorously attacked those heaps of loose dirt.

And it was Carmella who, later, breathlessly leaning on the shovel, looking round in surprise, called Olds' attention to the absence of the Indian.

"He'll turn up," Barney said indifferently. "That's the trouble with Injuns — you gotta watch 'em every minute." He finished tramping the fill, got a greasewood switch and brushed out their tracks, then stepped back, carefully anchoring in his mind enough of the landmarks to be sure of the site. "We better git on back before the dang jigger takes it into his noggin t' make off with the horses."

But the horses were there; the packs took a bit of finding but they hadn't been rifled. Charlie wasn't in evidence but they could see where he'd built himself a fire, a pretty good-sized one.

"What did he want with a *fire?*" Carmella asked, puzzled stare searching Barney's.

Olds shrugged, but it was plain he didn't like it. "Guess we might's well eat," he said to her finally and, going over to the packs, dug out several cans.

"Couldn't we celebrate tonight and have a real meal?"

Barney said brashly, "Why not?" and she got at it.

They were eating when Charlie put in a belated resurrection. Olds, eyeing him narrowly, waved at the grub. "Draw up your butt an' squat," he invited.

"No hungry," the old man grunted.

Olds went on with his eating. When he was finished Charlie beckoned him aside. "Give squaw now!"

Olds, getting red in the face, swelled up. Before he could lubricate his throat enough to get words out of it the Pima demanded: "You ketchum whiskey?"

"No!" Olds snarled. "*Now* — you pipe down before I swarm all over you! We had a

192

deal. The deal still stands, but it don't include that girl you're oglin' so git yer eyes off her."

The Indian looked at him hard as stone, spun suddenly around and went stalking off. In a couple of minutes a wild rush of hoofs tore away from where Olds had earlier hobbled the stock.

Carmella stood up. "What was that all about?"

"Nothin' fer you t' worry about," Barney grumbled. "That ol' coot gives himself more airs'n a dang sheepherder! He'll git over it, I expect. Don't make no never-mind t' me either way. Whiskey! I'll 'whiskey' him, by godfreys, if he gits smart with *me!*"

He looked again at the sky, more disturbed than he let on. It lacked a good couple hours till dark yet the sun hanging low over Cottonwood Hill appeared to be settling into smoke. The air was close and still and everything had a yellow-green look which reminded him uncomfortably of the night they'd quit Grant. Unless his arm was considerably mistaken they were going to have wind before this night was over.

XXV

They got it, too.

More dang wind than a man could know what to do with. Gusts and gales that crammed the air with flying crystals, wailing off ridges, screaming around rocks and leaving Olds feeling like some son of a bitch had been after him with sandpaper. When it finally quit he was raw all over, every inch of him scraped and pumiced like a wagon being readied for a new coat of paint. And not one peep had Carmella turned loose. She had more damn guts than you could hang on a fencepost!

Peering at her in the dawn's chilly light it came over him suddenly that whichever fool had give out women was the frailer sex simply didn't know what he was talking about. She looked cold and pinched and considerable bedraggled but still could show that gamin grin. It made Olds feel ten years older than Methuselah when he resentfully stood up to stare across the drifted sand that now lay over everything like a fall of snow. "What's t' grin at?" he growled, scowling.

She was even able to laugh!

Olds did grin finally, a disgusted grimace. "Them horses is prob'ly halfway t' China!"

and she wisely kept still while he stomped around grumbling, full of blather and bluster.

"Don't you think," the girl asked, "we should be looking for that chimney?"

He did, indeed. It had been in his mind. The only way he could rationalize the reluctance he felt to get at it was by acknowledging the creeping fear in him that they'd no longer be able to find the cursed ledge.

The packs were gone, ripped apart and scattered by that goddam wind. To persons unfamiliar with the violence of desert storms this might seem hard to swallow, but all Olds could unearth after digging through the drifts was half a dozen tins of heavily salted bully beef.

At least they wouldn't starve, because he didn't aim to stay here any longer than it took to place the markers the law required. Always providing, he thought morosely, all the things he'd taken bearing from weren't plumb buried under sand.

To protect their title the find had to be recorded and the nearest available place was Tucson, more than sixty miles away.

With the cleaned and loaded repeater in hand, Olds' most pressing need was to locate the horses but, as he'd strongly suspected, these were not where he'd left them. Though they devoted the best part of an hour to the search the only luck they had was to finally discover Pammy and one of the pack mules, both with their hobbles gone.

Pammy, at least, appeared delighted to see them and set up a monstrous racket to prove it. Olds reckoned the Indian, before he'd gone off, had cut the stock loose out of spite. It was God's plain mercy he hadn't cut their throats.

"See," Carmella said cheerfully, "we're not as bad off as you thought we were."

Olds grunted sourly. "Get aboard," he grumbled. "It's the quickest way back."

"How can we steer them without reins or halter?"

But they made out, though he stopped back at camp to kick through the drifts again, fruitlessly. "Guess we might's well divide one of these cans," Olds said. "Apt t' be some while before we'll have any chance to line our stomachs again."

It was eleven o'clock — actually somewhat after — before they were ready to set out for the chimney. Carmella was all for riding. Olds didn't want to track up the landscape. But when she said, "How do you figure to make them stay hitched?" he had to agree, having nothing to tie them with, that maybe they had better take them along. Pammy could be depended on to stay in their vicinity but that jug-headed mule was something else again. "You'll hev t' keep your eye on him — hell, mebbe you better ride him," Olds growled, and set off afoot, the burro docilely following.

But they hadn't gone far before he pulled up to stare, knuckling his eyes with a bewildered fist. Carmella stared too, astonished at what the force of that gale had accomplished during the night. For nearly two miles the big ridge they'd traveled had completely disappeared, buried beneath a fluted sea of drifted sand. Stark and glittering it lay, unmarked by a single track, majestic as some awful terrain glimpsed through a lunar glass.

Olds swore under the crushing weight of this defeat.

To find Yuma's chimney only to lose it this way seemed almost worse than never seeing it at all. How long they stared Olds had no way of knowing. It must have been a good while, each of them sunk in bitter gloom, stopped cold by what must have seemed insurmountable catastrophe. The sun was straight overhead when the girl at last, timidly, plucked at Barney's sleeve. He looked at her like he'd been walking in his sleep.

"Maybe," she said, "the gulch wasn't buried."

"Not buried!" Olds snarled. "You don't see it, do you?"

"Well, there's something off there. . . ." She pointed. "Don't you see where it looks as though the sand drops away? Off there beyond that darker patch — see?"

Barney blew out his breath in a kind of moan. "That ain't where the gulch was."

"How do you know?" Carmella persisted. "We're probably all turned around."

He looked back toward where they had spent the night, unable to find the place. He could see their tracks though, the ones they'd just made getting over to this point. Seeming puzzled again he irritably scratched at his jaw. It did sort of look like he'd got mixed up *some*place. He couldn't work up much hope for it but guessed they hadn't much to lose, beyond what time it would take them to get over there. "C'mon," he grumbled.

It wasn't a great deal farther than it actually looked but the view was deceptive. The sand was loose, not yet packed down. Every step Olds took he went in to the ankles. The animals went deeper. And it was almost as hard to get out of as flypaper. It took them nearly two hours to reach the point Carmella had thought might be an end of the stuff.

The blue mule's hide was dark with sweat, time it fetched the girl up to Olds and stopped. It was plain straightaway she had been right about the sand — it did end here, or perhaps this was where the big blow had first let go of it, filling up all the hollows, leveling everything off until what they'd come through most resembled the bed of some vanished sea.

"You sick or something?" She peered at him anxiously.

Olds did look to be in a sure enough trance, eyes poked out like knobs on a stick. Made her feel kind of funny herself, but not near as queer as the jolt she got when, turning her head, she followed his stare. With her jaw dropped open she turned pale as a ghost.

It was the gulch that lay before them, but deeper, scoured clean, stripped of brush. And rising sheer as a butte against the far slope's stone ribs stood Yuma's chimney, awe inspiring, nakedly beautiful as a pillar of fire.

A far-off shout winging over the sand jerked

them out of their dreams, brought them wheeling to face the hard realities of a cruel and treacherous combination of foes.

Back there at the far edge of this blanket of sand they could see a drawn-up huddle of gesticulating horsemen. Even as they watched, these broke apart to come spurring toward them, waving rifles.

Not until the van of those larruping riders struck the fluted swirls of this drifted sand and lost their momentum did Olds, apparently stunned, move out of his tracks. Then "C'mon," he yelled, "let's git outa here!" A snarl peeled back his whisker-stubbled lips. "Here — you take Pammy. I'll ride the mule."

The switch completed, Carmella whirled the burro toward concealment down below this cap of freshly moved sand.

"Cris' sake — not down there!" Olds cursed. "We want t' pull 'em away from that chimney — foller me!"

There wasn't much use trying to hustle the animals through this kind of stuff. A wallowing walk was the best they could manage, but that bunch coming after them couldn't do any better without ruining their horses, and they soon found it out. Looking back across a shoulder Olds could see one of them changing direction, and now the

200

whole push was strung out after him, swinging to come up on a tangent, hoping to cut down the fugitives' lead.

"Better run along the rim fer a ways," he told Carmella, and the footing there did seem a little firmer. "We better save these critters all we can till we git outa this," he called back abruptly and, keeping hold of an ear, jumped off the big mule to jog along beside it. Carmella, grimacing, got off old Pammy.

To keep Sully's crew from catching sight of the chimney they were forced to head for the place where the ridge came up out of this sand. They weren't much more than half a mile from it and for a while they seemed to be holding their own. But the pursuit, catacornering across their course, though having farther to go were also better mounted, and by the time Barney and the girl got free of the sand they looked a lot nearer. "Where," Olds growled, "does this ridge go to?"

Carmella didn't know. "Probably drops down into the desert," she guessed. This was likewise Barney's conclusion; but hoping to win back some of their lost lead while they had decent footing — enough anyway to keep them free of Shinnan's guns until dark could even the odds a little, he had the girl mount up and hauled himself astride the mule.

The ridge, more thickly grown to greasewood here, played out inside of a mile. Olds twisted a look at the sun with clamped jaws. For the moment at least they were out of sight and the desert hereabouts was heavily studded with silver-spined cholla, much of it tall as a mounted man, which would force Sullivan's outfit to stay with their tracks a good part of the time.

Looking round again he guessed their best bet was to make for the mountains, the footslopes of which were scarcely two miles away. He kicked the mule into a run, Pammy thudding after him. If they stuck to these flats there was bound to be gunplay. Once into the mountains there would be less chance of that; with luck they might elude the pursuit altogether.

They held to their pace for another half hour. If that bunch behind hadn't yet quit the sand Olds thought he and the girl should have a pretty fair chance of keeping clear until dark in this cut-up country along the base of the mountains. When they reached the foothills and paused to rest the mule and burro it was Carmella who put the whole rub in a nutshell.

She said, wearily pushing the hair off

damp cheeks, "If we can get through these mountains and push straight to Tucson there's a pretty fair chance we'll come out of this alive."

"Sure," he growled, "but we got t' put up monuments! Minin' law —"

She looked at him bitterly. "What good are monuments to a couple of dead fools?"

"We ain't dead yet!"

"You're the stubbornest short-eared mule I've met! Be reasonable, Barney. We haven't a dog's chance of getting back to that chimney and coming away from it again. There's too many of them — we don't even know we saw the whole lot!"

They were letting the animals blow again. Olds for a moment considered her squarely, seeing the drawn cheeks, the fullness of her — the things this woman could give to a man, and he gnashed his teeth. But he'd put five years into finding that gold and the thought of leaving it was more than he could stand.

She could see this in his stiffening shoulders. She took a deep breath. "There's more than one way of skinning a cat. Once we've got to Tucson and filed, who's to say that bunch of crooks didn't simply move in and tear up our notices?"

Olds thought about it. "You mean just go on?"

"It wouldn't be the first time a claim's been jumped."

Barney had to shake his head. "You're fergittin' King George. He's got that town plumb jammed in his pocket, an' the town marshall too! It wouldn't work anyway. We couldn't make it stick. The man on the ground has everythin' goin' fer him. I can tell you this: we leave 'em in possession they'll *stay* in possession. An' possession, by God, is nine points in the law."

Her eyes stabbed him dourly. "So even if we go back and put up the markers one of us will have to stay there — is that it?"

He nodded.

"Then we're whipped," she said flatly. "Oh, why can't you admit —"

"We ain't whipped yet!"

About to kick his mule into motion, Olds seemed abruptly almost to stop breathing. Head to one side, the whole look of him stiffening, his gimlet eyes raked the slopes ahead. Carmella's cheeks went gray as she too, then, caught the strengthening pound of oncoming hoofs.

XXVI

No crystal ball could have told Barney plainer this was no one — but nobody — he craved to meet. No friends were going to yank him out of the frying pan. Whoever was coming could only add to his problems and decrease the slim chance he was trying to believe he still had.

"You go ahead — try t' make it t' Tucson," he growled, whacking Pammy toward those harsh gray steepening knobs folks called mountains, at the same time wheeling his reluctant mule into the brush that fringed an uninviting drop to the desert.

But, despite his quick thinking, they were not to escape scot-free because Carmella, once again, displayed a mind of her own. Whirling the confused burro, she came ramming after Olds just as the horsebackers burst into view.

They reined up, startled, peering, unconcealably astonished. But only for an instant. A sharp yell was wrung from their leader. With a shout the whole push, unlimbering rifles, put spurs to their horses.

Barney caught one clear look at that black-hatted rider in the van of this outfit and bitterly cursing sent his mule tearing through the slap of branches.

Rifles cracked out a ragged volley. Slugs clipped twigs as they ripped through the brush; one cuffed Barney's hat, another fetched a snort from the lumbering mule.

Olds could hear Pammy crashing through the growth behind but the girl's predicament didn't move him to stop. That black-hatter bugger was the grubstake king who had squared all his bills for the past five years and Olds wasn't waiting around for no chat. His dearest hope was to someway get clear, and if the girl didn't make it — well, that was just too bad.

The mule tried to swerve when he saw the drop but Barney gave him no chance. He cracked the big walloper across the butt with his rifle and the mule shot over the rim braying frantically.

A horse at that pace might have got Barney killed but the mule never lost his balance once. Back on his haunches he rode that slide like a sure-enough surfer all the roaring terrifying way to the bottom. And Pammy, groaning like a rusty gate, wasn't about to be outdone by no dang mule no matter *how* big he was.

Olds was off the mule's back and lifting his Henry before the last loosened rock went bounding past. He lined up his sights, gauging breeze and trajectory, so that when the first horse was hauled up on the lip it was no task at all to tighten finger on trigger. He shot straight off, saw the rider explode sideways and, still trying to stop himself, come teetering over the crumbling rim. No one else was so brash.

The man Olds had nailed lodged against a bush partway down and hung there limp as a wrung-out dishrag. Olds was only sorry the guy wasn't Sullivan, because nothing but a slug would ever get 'Lucky' George off his back — he knew that much.

When Carmella, round-eyed, let out a shocked protest Barney never bothered even to glance around. Still with scrinched stare quartering that lip he grumbled through clenched teeth, "Sure, you don't hev t' tell me. I know I'm chicken! Instead of goin' fer a leg I oughta busted his surcingle — I meant to, dang it. I just funked out."

"You — you mean he isn't dead?"

"Naw, he's playin' possum," Olds growled, finally lowering his weapon when after waiting three minutes nobody else showed. "They're huntin' another way down. We better make tracks."

Nudging Pammy after him Carmella called presently, "How do you suppose those fellows got up there ahead of us?"

"Diff'rent bunch. Gink in the black bonnet was Sully — yep, the ol' he-walrus himself, dang his eyes! Figgered t' catch us between two fires. I'll smash his plans yet if we kin stay clear till dark."

They did win clear but it took considerable dashing around, and Olds wasn't sure even then he had lost them. Twice more they'd exchanged running shots with that group and the last time — to make sure they got the message — Olds had dropped three horses.

Then, just before night flung down its welcoming blanket, they had run headlong into Fek Shinnan's crew which had obviously been laying for them. Olds' mule was hit and the girl took a nasty burn across the bulge of one hip.

Olds was so incensed he shot Goyanno out of the saddle and worked the lever till his repeater was shot dry, tumbling Shinnan's horse on the final squeeze. The rest of them, ere that, had took off in a dozen directions and Barney, if the big mule hadn't been so damn spooked, would have had more shells stuffed into the loader tube and nailed Shinnan sure.

But the mule, stampeding, took him out of range before he could get his piece in operation. Might be it was just as well because it soon became plain, even to him, the girl stood in need of attention. She was leaking blood like a dang stuck pig and her eyes looked like holes burnt in a wagon sheet.

He stopped quick as they had pulled out of sight. She was plenty game, insisting they keep on, but her voice didn't sound too convincing to Olds. He got her off the burro and — red in the face as a San Ildefonso squaw on a snootful of Taos lightning — got enough of her clothes pushed out of the way to tell what he'd got to deal with.

He could see right away it wasn't nothing to get up no sweat about so long as it was tended and she didn't pass out. Painful, of course — an ugly three-inch gash about a quarter inch deep — but the blood she was losing was the biggest drawback. Seeming all thumbs and copiously sweating, he got it washed out the best he could, and wrapped some padding in place with a couple strips torn off some kind of underthing. Then he looked at the mule and did some real sweating.

Be goddam lucky if it lasted two miles!

Peering through the darkening air he didn't see anything that held out much hope. Ought to put the animal out of its misery but they just couldn't shorten their chances. Even in the night you could mostly see pretty good on the desert — a heap *too* good if you were attempting to hide from the sort of codgers Sullivan had in his string. Nope. They'd simply got to keep going for as long as they could and trust the good Lord to dredge up a miracle.

The wind was getting pretty lively again. He hoped that spill had broke Goyanno's neck. He was reasonably sure the smuggler was done up for *this* fight — he'd gone off that horse like a sack of potatoes. Olds was sorry he hadn't got Shinnan as well — and old Charlie! He had seen the old devil on his paint horse with Sully and wasted two shots trying to settle his hash. At least those buggers would be more cautious for a while — he hoped.

Stars came out but there wasn't any moon; Barney took what comfort he was able from this, but the wind kept rising and he was filled with disquiet, almost a foreboding. By morning, anyway, it would have hidden their tracks but he was bitterly afraid with Charlie along they wouldn't need any tracks to guess where he was bound. Olds had to get back and rock that claim.

Out of the long silence Carmella, always practical, asked: "How much will it cost to get that gold out?"

"A pack string of mules or burros would do it if we worked it ourselfs," Barney grunted.

"A hundred and twenty miles each trip."

Barney, dismally, gauging the run of her thoughts, said, "We could prob'ly hire guards . . . some of them Yaquis, mebbe, that's driftin' up outa Mexico. Give 'em plenty of beef an' a .30-30 apiece —"

"And the next thing you know there'll be a sheriff riding after us."

Olds said, blustering: "A man's got a right t' defend . . ." and let it go. Against George Sullivan you had no rights at all. This country was run to suit the haves. The biggest have was Lucky George, and everybody knew it.

Olds continued to brood on injustice in general but mostly on the wrongs which were frustrating him. The longer he brooded the more convinced he became that their only real out was a bullet with George's name carved into its nose.

The mule collapsed under him, Olds barely vaulting clear, some ten minutes later. With the water sack looped across his shoulder, Henry in hand, Olds plodded on through the starlit night, Pammy following like a dog at his heels.

It looked pretty hopeless. Anyone else

might have quit, but Olds was tough as a white oak post. He'd get the best of George yet — or know the reason why.

Near midnight — that wind was really rough now — Barney and the girl dropped down into a hollow to get some relief and give the burro a breather. Olds whacked open the last of the tinned beef and they washed it down gloomily with a couple of swallows apiece from their dwindling water. Olds, emptying the rest of it into his hat, stood fuming and fretting while the burro, in no discernible hurry, delicately lowered it and then made ready to chew up his head-gear.

Olds helped Carmella to get mounted again, then, jaws clamped, chin on chest, strode bitterly into the teeth of the wind. But the storm before long got too bad to buck and they were forced to pull off into a stand of mesquite where they spent a miserable couple of hours waiting out the worst of it before, in sheer desperation, he got them moving once more.

"How do you figure to get into that gulch?" the girl sufficiently roused to call presently. "Are you trying to get back to where we first saw that bunch?"

Olds shook his head. "I'm hopin' t' come onto the far end of it. We're north of it now, near as I kin reckon."

"Do you suppose Charlie told them about that chimney?"

This was something Barney had been wooling around himself. "Don't seem too likely," he finally grumbled. "Firewater's what that ol' sinner really wants. Prob'ly bargained t' put 'em on our trail fer a bottle."

He said after a moment, "Even if George wormed it out of him we was huntin' that formation — an' with Goyanno in tow he already knew that — I don't expect Charlie would've told him we'd come onto anythin'. He could see we was diggin' but, from where he was, he sure as hell couldn't see *what* we got hold of. Anyway these Injuns is superstitious about mines — they know what gold kin do to a country."

She didn't say anything more and Olds was too far down in the dumps to put any effort into time-passing chitchat. Try as he would he could discover no way by which he and Carmella were like to come out on top. Not this time, not against the odds George had marshaled against them. Olds might win a few skirmishes, a few trifling hands, but when the chips were down it was bound to be Sullivan who picked up the pot.

■ ■ ■ ■

In chill, still windy, earliest light Barney
stopped and peered back at the girl to growl
grumpily: "We made it. The gulch is just
over that rise there, yonder."

The girl wearily lifted red-rimmed eyes to
stare where he pointed, too beat for talk.

"You all right?" he said.

"I guess so." She scrubbed a hand across
sand-roughened cheeks and then, still staring, breathlessly croaked: "Barney — look!"

Olds whirled, and cursed.

Far out, across the gray dun of these
desolate wastes where sand met sky in a
hogbacked horizon, a thin file of dark
shapes were climbing into view, wheeling
out upon the ridge two by two in precise
formation. "Cavalry!" Barney snarled, seeing the guidon at their head.

"I guess," Carmella mentioned with a
faint twist of smile, "the Lord must have
heard you."

Barney glared at her in outrage.

"But don't you see," she cried, "that
crowd won't dare pull anything wild with
soldiers around!"

It took some getting used to, for Olds, like
most of this country's denizens, was not ac-

customed to imagining anything good ever could come out of a military presence. But he began to feel gradually that maybe this time a patrol in the vicinity might be of some use. Sullivan had no strings on the Army; in Feltenmeyer's eyes he was a money-grubbing crook.

"I believe they see us. . . ."

Barney, still dubious, reckoned they did. "C'mon," he grumbled, "let's git that claim rocked."

And broke into a run, time nagging him again. Just because he did not see any of that bunch was no proof at all Shinnan and the grubstake king had got lost. But when Olds came panting up onto the rise he found nothing beyond it but unbroken sand with never a bush, stob or rock to break the bleak view.

He stared, jaw dropped, incredulous. In a cold sweat, aghast, he searched the terrain for the bearings he'd taken, the knob tops and ranges.

Yes — he could see Malpais Hill and, off there against the skyline, Crozier Peak — even the tip of Lookout Mountain. Every check point showed, smack-dab where they should be — he hadn't been mistaken. But the gulch was gone. Even the place where they had camped — gone like a ciphering sponged from a boy's slate, deep buried under tons of drifted sand. Two million dollars worth of gold!

He damned near cried.

"Well . . . where is it?" Carmella asked; and all he could say was: *That goddam wind!*

The girl touched his sleeve. "There's Sullivan and company."

Olds, drained of hope, tiredly twisted his head to scan the advance of the ragged swash of horsebackers crow-hopping their mounts across that fresh spread of sand, the frock-coated, black-hatted grubstake king well out in front with his trouble-shooting hardcase, the hook-nosed Fek Shinnan.

Even as Olds looked they began to spread out, unlimbering rifles, as though determined to make sure he didn't slip them again. And just about then the cavalry patrol climbed into sight behind their guidon and scouts, Colonel Feltenmeyer himself spearheading the command.

Lucky George pulled up, frowning, and then — apparently thinking better of it — came on with his hired killer, ironing out his face into a semblance of reasonable annoyance as the irascible colonel, quitting his troop, rode up onto the bench from the opposite side.

Feltenmeyer got in the first word, demanding with some asperity: "What's going on here? Inform me, sir! I should like to know the occasion for this warlike show of arms!"

Lucky George, appearing cool as a well chain, met the colonel's glower with an easy smile. "I expect," he said, "they're a little apprehensive. And not without reason." He darted a cold stare at Barney. "We've been trying to come up with this feller for two days. Each time I've attempted to hail him the fool cuts loose with that Henry repeater. He crippled four horses yesterday and knocked a man out of the saddle."

"Yeah — it's too bad about him! Too bad I didn't kill him!" Olds threw back belligerently.

"You see?" Sullivan said with a spread of hands. "The feller's incorrigible! Have you any idea," the man asked seriously, "how much this joker has cost me, Colonel?"

"Eh? Cost you?"

"Aye. Cost me! Five years, through good times and poor, I, Lucky George, have supported this wastrel in his search for that chimney, and I say in all humility it has cost me a fortune. Can you blame me for wanting to get some of it back?"

"Well . . ." The probing, harsh stare of the

217

discountenanced officer fastened on Olds in a disheartening manner. "Have you anything to say?"

"That jasper I shot — you want know who it was?"

The colonel said rather curtly: "Would it make any difference?"

"Don't guess that's fer me t' say, sir. This girl here kin tell —"

"It was Peep Goyanno," Carmella spoke up.

"That smuggler!" Feltenmeyer's darkening glance swept like a thunderclap back to George Sullivan, distrustful, censorious, bristling with questions.

But the grubstake king was not caught out. "So that's who he was. I'm not too surprised. He came into my camp off the desert, half out of his head with sun and thirst. Called himself Sanchez — said he'd been in Olds' party, that Olds had stripped him of horse, guns and water. Said Olds was bound for the old Arivaipa camp where he was to meet a Pima Indian with supplies from Winkelman — that Olds had found Yuma's Chimney and was going to file claim to it."

Olds told his side of it. The Colonel didn't seem to know whom to believe. He finally said to Sullivan: "Do you intend to press charges?"

"Oh, I think we can settle this amicable," Sully smiled. "After paying all this rascal's bills for five —"

"I thought I saw in the papers you were disclaiming —"

"Well . . . yes," Sullivan frowned. "But the fact that he's *found* this gold rather changes the complection of the whole matter, doesn't it? This Pima who fetched in supplies for him subsequently fled in fear of his life — he was in the gulch when Olds uncovered it. Told me he saw Barney Olds and the girl —"

"All right," Feltenmeyer growled. "Make your point."

"I think it's well taken. I believe any jury in the country, once the facts are properly presented, will consider it most likely Olds made this strike earlier, deliberately concealing his discovery until his grubstake contracts with me had expired. Doesn't it appear to you uncommonly peculiar that as soon as I publicly wash my hands of him he comes out here prepared to find and stake this claim?"

The Colonel made a business of clearing his throat. "We don't actually know — at least it isn't apparent — that he's found anything at all."

"It's apparent enough to me," Sullivan said, blackly scowling. "I can produce an Indian — that Pima I mentioned — that saw him uncover the top of that chimney! Why don't you search him? He must have taken samples —"

"Y'mean like this?" Barney said, tossing the man the lump of ore Carmella had taken from the White Horse Bar.

"There!" cried the grubstake king with satisfaction. "What did I tell you! I can prove conclusively this chunk of ore came off that lost ledge!"

"How?" asked the colonel, distastefully frowning in the pervading effluvium of unwashed bodies. "I mean, without you've got the ledge —"

"In my office at Tucson I've several bonafide pieces of the ore removed from that chimney by McLean and Crittenden. . . ."

"I suppose you have some kind of proposition?"

"Yes," Lucky George said, "I'll buy him out."

"Fer how much?" Olds growled.

"A hundred thousand dollars."

"Why you parsimonious two-bit crook! That gold," Barney snarled, "is worth a cool three million —"

"It will be worth a lot less," Sully grinned through his teeth, "after lawyers and the courts get done wrangling over it. You'd better take what I offer and settle this now."

"I'll sell you *my* half for one hundred thousand," Carmella spoke up.

"*Your* half!" Lucky George looked somewhat taken aback.

The girl dug a bully beef label from her shirt, presented it to the colonel, Sullivan crowding up to read across his shoulder. "Seems to be in order," Feltenmeyer observed.

"Fifty thousand," Sullivan said, but the girl was adamant.

"All right," Sully growled after considerable soul searching, "I'll give you the hundred if you can prove to me you know where it's at."

The girl dug the tobacco tin out of her clothes and passed it to the colonel who removed the paper from its hiding place and read aloud: "Twenty-third October, eighteen sixty. McLean and Crittenden."

That really got to George. You could see the hook going in. Still he stood there, fingering his watch chain, nervously considering.

It wasn't that he trusted them — he never trusted anyone, but greed got the better of him. It must have crossed his mind that Olds, in front of witnesses this way, would be a lot less likely to indulge his bad habits; and, besides, he wasn't dealing with Olds.

"You're on!" he snapped. But, still suspicious, halfway glowering, he prissily added, "Providing, of course, I'm put in touch with it."

Carmella smiled. "You can have Charlie show you. I'll write out the location, giving my word the gold is actually there. But I'll want the colonel to —"

"My dear," the old dodderer declared, fatuously grinning, "I'm yours to command."

"Wait a second," Barney grumbled. "I ain't fixin' t' git saddled with no pardner like you! You kin buy me out, too —"

"We can talk about that," Lucky George said nastily, "when the mine is in production. Now what's this about the colonel?"

Folding the paper the girl gave him back his silver-plated pencil. Handing the paper then to Feltenmeyer she said, "I'd like for you to hold this — and him, if you don't mind — until tomorrow noon. Just to make sure there are no unpleasant surprises."

Sullivan scowled.

"Come, man," the colonel pressed, "you surely aren't questioning the word of a lady?

Her sworn statement in writing!"

The grubstake king, muttering, wrote out his check. Feltenmeyer, after scanning it, passed it to the girl. "We'll be going back to Grant," he informed her, pulling on his gauntlets. "About detaining this . . . ah, gentleman. Do you feel tomorrow noon will really be long enough?"

"That feller," Olds put in with a grumble, "would skin a flea fer its hide an' taller — I want t' git that banked before he finds some way t' chisel us outa it!"

"Yes," Carmella smiled with a fond look. "You see, Barney has decided that we — he and I — will be traveling life's highway together from here out. Noontime tomorrow will be just fine. We'll locate a preacher first thing in the morning. Then we'll take Sully's check to the bank."

We hope you have enjoyed this Large Print book. Other Thorndike, Wheeler, Kennebec, and Chivers Press Large Print books are available at your library or directly from the publishers.

For information about current and upcoming titles, please call or write, without obligation, to:

Publisher
Thorndike Press
10 Water St., Suite 310
Waterville, ME 04901
Tel. (800) 223-1244

or visit our Web site at:

http://gale.cengage.com/thorndike

OR

Chivers Large Print
published by AudioGO Ltd
St James House, The Square
Lower Bristol Road
Bath BA2 3SB
England
Tel. +44(0) 800 136919
email: info@audiogo.co.uk
www.audiogo.co.uk

All our Large Print titles are designed for easy reading, and all our books are made to last.